Kora's Choice

A Paradise Series Story

IVANA L. TRUGLIO

JONQUIL
PRESS

For my mother, Maria Truglio
who bought me every book I ever asked for and more!

ABOUT THE AUTHOR

Ivana lives in Sydney, Australia. She devotes most, if not all, of her spare time to writing the Paradise Series.

She studied aviation, archaeology and ancient history at university. During her studies, it was rumoured that she lived in the university library. She currently holds a private pilot licence and rides a motorbike.

Ivana is married and has two young children who reap the benefits of having a mother with a wild imagination. She has been writing since she was a child and the characters in the Paradise Series have been living in her head for over 15 years.

ACKNOWLEDGEMENTS

My first thanks goes to my editor, Anicee Dowling, not only for being the best editor I've ever had, but also for making the brilliant suggestion of writing a back story for one of my characters.

A big thanks to my writing group who helped *Kora's Choice* find its feet during a turbulent Camp NaNoWriMo.

Lastly, I'd like to thank my husband and children who never seem to mind just how much time I spend writing my stories. I particularly like the times when my son watched over my shoulder and read aloud as I wrote.

Chapter One

Kora walked straight to her room and shut herself in. She rarely locked the door – usually she didn't mind visitors – but today she turned the key *twice*, took the key out of the lock. Her fingers trembled as she placed the key on the small table by the tall, thin window. She gripped them with her other hand only to realise she was shaking all over.

The door rattled, and she heard a frustrated huffing. Someone knocked loudly at the door. Kora turned and almost went to open it, out off pure habit, but stopped. Today, she didn't want to talk to anyone. She was owed one evening of solitude after what her family had endured.

"Kora, open up!" Nyssa shouted impatiently at her from the hall. When Kora didn't answer, her sister banged harder on the door. "Kora, let me in!"

"No," she said quietly, frustrated that Nyssa wouldn't leave her alone. They didn't need to spend *more* time with each other. Not after what they'd had to do together.

Kora felt a familiar mind touch hers. Grinding her teeth, she pushed out with her power and forced her sister away.

"Don't. Do. That," Kora said every word slowly and calmly. She did not feel calm – not at all – but she did not want Nyssa to go crying to their father. He had enough to deal with, and Nyssa's dramatics would only make it worse.

"You aren't the only one who lost someone, you know?" Nyssa cried out from the hallway.

"Neither are you," Kora pointed out. "I'm allowed to close my door, just like father did. What you do is up to you."

"Ugh!" Nyssa stamped her foot so hard on the carpeted floor that Kora could hear it from behind her door. After a moment, Kora sent a tiny tendril of power under her door, searching for her sister. She breathed a sigh of relief when she realised she was gone.

She shrugged her heavy rucksack off her stiff shoulders and unceremoniously dumped it on the floor, next to the table. There was nothing in there that mattered. Not anymore. She tried so hard to block her thoughts, not only from the rest of the castle, but also from herself.

A bath, she told herself. *A bath to wash away the dirt.*

And the blood. The thought rose unbidden.

She looked down at her arms. They were still streaked with blood. There hadn't been time to wash it off. In their haste to get home, to Illaria, the three of them had wrapped the bodies in their cloaks and woven their power together to carry the four bodies – her mother, two brothers and little sister. Kora blinked back tears at the image of Adina's tiny, lifeless form.

No, she pushed it away. *Not now. I need a bath.*

In the bathroom adjoining her bedroom, she used her power to drag water up the pipes into her bath before plunging the plug into the drain. She *knew* she wasn't meant to use her power to draw her own bath, not until her teachers had given her clearance. However, the number of things she'd done on the return trip that were forbidden without guidance were too many to count, and she doubted one more infraction would be noticed. Not now, when the castle would be in complete chaos.

With barely any effort, she lit the fireplace and drew heat from it to warm the bath water as she stripped off her clothes. They were caked with mud and blood. She didn't know whose. Adina and Fredryck had been the worst, but Vaughn and their mother hadn't looked much better by the time they died.

Stop! She caught herself up again. *Just stop thinking of them. Hop into the bath, wash away the dirt ...*

and the blood ...

and put on some nice clean clothes.

She stepped into the bath and sank down until she was fully submerged. She ducked her head out of the water again to see that it was already murky from the mud. Distressed that she could not clean the water with a wave of her hands, the way she had seen the elves do, Kora drained the bath and filled it again without getting out. She scrubbed her skin until it felt raw but, clean as the rest of her was, she could not get rid of the blood beneath her fingernails. Kora climbed out of the bath quicker than she would have liked.

The soft, light towels absorbed whatever remained on her skin. Not wanting to put her hand back in, she used her power to take the plug out and watched the brownish-red water drain away.

She dropped the stained towels in the bath. She didn't care that the maids would be unimpressed. What did it matter what anyone thought of her?

At least it's better than leaving it to stain the sandstone floor, the abstract thought entered her mind unbidden. She knew how stains soaked into sandstone and rarely came out. She did not need bloodied sandstone as permanent reminder.

She dressed quickly and carelessly in whatever her hand touched first.

Does it matter what I wear? Will that ever *matter again*?

Chapter Two

It was too hot. She could feel the sun beating down and burning her skin as she stood at the door of the cavern, waiting for the bodies of her mother, brothers and little sister to reach them. Uncle Lukys had taken care of the arrangements. Her father had ... not been in a state of mind to do anything in the days since their return.

Kora risked a glance at him. Her father's face was pale and drawn, and he looked like he had aged years in the span of a week. His haggard appearance may have drawn sympathy from the Illarians, but Kora had little left for him. She and Nyssa had lost just as much as he had, but they still had to carry on. Kora was the one ensuring her father took a daily walk around the gardens to get him out of his room, much as she wanted to stay in her own. Kora was the one ringing the bell for his food. She doubted he would have thought to do it even once if she hadn't done it for him.

Kora had been the one who had to tell Uncle Lukys everything that had happened, and where, so that he could send out guards to make sure the humans were dealt with accordingly. She did not want to think what they would do if they found the murderers. There was already hatred enough for lintep in the Outworld. Would they make it worse?

Beside her father stood Nyssa. *She* hadn't really been much help. Nyssa was too busy drinking up all the sympathy their family and her friends had to offer. With a small shrug, Kora had to admit she was glad no one was knocking on *her* door to offer condolences. She *hated* dealing with that. She didn't want to hear how much others missed her family. It couldn't bring them back and it most certainly did not make her feel better to hear it. She would rather grieve for her family in private. If she could have, she would have skipped the entire interment and gone down to the cavern by herself another day.

I wish, she thought as the coffins appeared through the crowd, borne on the shoulders of lintep guards. Much as she had loved her mother and brothers, Adina's coffin was the one which brought tears to her eyes. It was so small – much smaller than any coffin should be.

Kora looked away from the coffins, straight out into the crowd of people massed in the castle gardens. All eyes were on the funeral procession, with some people placing flowers on the coffins as they passed slowly by. Muffled sobs broke out in the silence but that was only to be expected. Her family was well loved in Illaria. There had been such high hopes for them. Now all that remained was a spoilt and powerful girl who breezed through her lessons without taking anything in or honing her skills, and a girl who disagreed with many of the teachings. It wasn't much to be left with. She looked over at her father with new eyes. Perhaps he *had* lost more than she and Nyssa. He had lost his wife and the only children who offered a promising future to the royal family.

The thought broke her heart just that little bit more. He must see her as such a disappointment. She'd always thought their heated debates over how lintep used their power was a welcome diversion for him. It hadn't occurred to her until just now that he might be disappointed in her views, especially now, given how their family had been murdered.

She blinked quickly, trying to stop the flow of tears. It didn't work. Hoping that no one would notice, she brushed away the tears from her cheeks, pretending to scratch her nose. It would attract sympathy that she did not want. She looked away from her father and the coffins again. She needed something to distract her. Something to calm her.

Unconsciously, she searched the crowd for a familiar face. One that she often sought out when she felt suffocated by her life. She had known Pér since they were young, but it was only in the last few years, since he joined classes in the castle, that she had begun to spend time with him. He had quickly made a place for himself in her extremely small circle of friends, Luisella and her cousins, Braedan and Aislen.

Pér often played songs for them on his lute. Just the memory of those songs made her smile. When he played, it always seemed as though things would be fine. She caught his eye in the crowd, but then it struck her that songs were just music and words. Songs could not bring her family back to life. She saw him frown. Even without reading her mind, she was certain he still knew what she was thinking. It felt like she was betraying him with that thought.

Beside her, Braedan gave her a little nudge. It was with guilty relief that she realised it was time to follow the coffins into the cavern. Uncle Lukys, Aislen, her father and Nyssa were already on their way. With a hurried step, she followed them down into the cavern.

She wasn't sure who was lighting the torches as they went, but she was grateful for the light. Even with the blue luminescent glow of the bitter oyster mushrooms, she knew she would have stumbled down the stone steps.

At the bottom of the cavern, Kora saw four graves dug out of the floor. She was glad they would all be buried next to each other, but it filled her with dread to look at the clear space next to those plots, knowing that it was now reserved for herself, Nyssa and their father.

"I can't do this," she whispered.

Aislen and Braedan were instantly by her side. They knew her well enough not to touch her skin. She *hated* it when people tried to manipulate her feelings through touch. Instead, Braedan lay an arm across her shoulders and pulled her in tight while Aislen squeezed her forearm.

"We've all of us buried a mother," Braedan whispered softly in her ear. "You've lost more than that, but we'll always be here for you."

"Always," whispered Aislen, giving her arm another squeeze.

Kora finally let out the tears she had been trying to hold back all morning. She found it odd that she felt safer now, in the suffocating cavern, than she had since her family was murdered.

Chapter Three

Kora sat through her lessons in a daze. She had barely slept the past week. Sleep brought vivid dreams of watching as her mother frantically pushed her shaking hands against the worst of Vaughn's wounds, crying in frustration and gasping in pain as she tried to save him.

Mistress Chandrelle had warned them many times that a lintep could only heal another person so much before they opened similar wounds on themselves. Vaughn had known, but she wasn't sure he understood the full consequences of his actions as he tried to save Fredryck. Their mother, however, knew full well what could happen.

Kora had stood silently with Nyssa and their father, watching in disbelief as her mother killed herself, trying to save a child who was beyond saving. None of them attempted to save her. Kora knew it would be impossible with wounds so bad. Perhaps the guilt from their sense of self-preservation was something they would all have to live with for the rest of their lives. Perhaps that was why her father had closeted himself in his room for the better part of every day.

It didn't help that the only times he had left his room and joined their extended family for dinner, Uncle Kynon reprimanded him for not doing *anything* to save his wife. Uncle Kynon had lost his own wife years ago, and it had left him very bitter. Kora knew he could not understand the three of them standing by and doing nothing.

Does he think we should have all died out there together? Kora thought angrily.

There was a sudden silence in the overly warm classroom. She looked up in surprise to see a ball of fire floating in front of her.

"An interesting interpretation of anger into fire, Kora, but not quite the skill we're practicing here today."

Kora extinguished the fire immediately with an apologetic glance at Master Flyndar.

"This is a prime example of why we cannot allow our emotions to rule us," Master Flyndar addressed the class at large. "We must practice self-control at all times or we risk unintentionally setting things on fire or worse."

"What's worse than unintentionally setting things on fire?" Gethin asked.

Kora grimaced. Gethin always tried to make her look bad. Master Flyndar walked around the room for a moment, seemingly lost in thought. Kora followed his movements, trying to ignore Gethin.

"Suppose there's a girl you like," he said, looking at Gethin. "She doesn't know you like her and you're too much of a coward to tell her how clever and skilful you think she is. You're too afraid that she might sneer at you for your lack of power or hopeless adoration of her."

Kora noticed some of the students shift uncomfortably. She fought to keep the smile off her face.

"Now," continued Master Flyndar, "imagine your fingers lightly brushing her arm in passing. You lose your self-control and all those thoughts fly from your mind straight to hers. Would *that* be worse than unintentionally setting something on fire?"

A few nervous laughs escaped from the students. Kora was rather beginning to enjoy herself. It wasn't often that arrogant students were put in their place. She wished it would happen more often.

"You should have seen the look on his face," Kora told Nerys as they walked together from class. "He went as white as chalk!"

Nerys laughed loudly. "I wish I hadn't been sitting behind him!"

"Don't be so cruel," Morewenna said quietly. "You don't know why he reacted like that."

"Who cares why?" Kora demanded, almost angrily. "He always tries to make me look bad. Am I not allowed to enjoy his *one* moment of discomfort?"

Without giving Morwenna a chance to reply, Kora stormed back to her chambers. She slammed the door and strode to the chaise. Frustrated with herself for continually losing her temper, she picked up a cushion and punched it repeatedly, then threw it across the room. The cushion hit Braedan in the face as he opened the door.

"Well, hello to you too," Braedan said, rubbing his nose as he bent to pick up the pillow. "Why do things always hit me right in the nose? They miss my ears, my fingers, any other extremity, but throw something at my face and it hits my nose every damn time!"

Kora sat on her chaise with a huff. "Sorry to have caused your nose such trouble, but when will you learn to knock?"

"Oh, probably never," Braedan answered nonchalantly as he fell into the seat next to her. He fiddled with the tassels on the cushion for a moment. "I saw Pér this morning in class. He said you haven't been to see him since you got back."

"I know," Kora replied tersely.

"Are you angry with him?"

Kora turned to her cousin, heart suddenly beating faster. "No. Is that what you think?"

Braedan shrugged. "It's certainly what Pér thinks. He said you looked at him once, just before the interment, and haven't spoken to him since – even in class."

"I'm not angry with *him*," Kora murmured, more to herself than to Braedan. Her cousin sat beside her a moment longer before standing up and leaning over so his face was level with hers.

"You *might* want to let him know that."

Kora threw the pillow at the door again as Braedan closed it behind himself.

Chapter Four

This is madness, she thought to herself as she padded quietly down the carpeted hall, shoes held in one hand. Her power was wrapped all around her, allowing her to blend into the background.

We practiced this for hours in the Outworld before...

She cut the thought off before it reached its conclusion. If she thought about that now, she would never get out of the palace undetected.

I should have gone to see him during the day! Like a normal person. But when have I ever been normal? Her critical thoughts nagged her, threatening to drag her spirits further down.

I should just go back to bed.

Kora looked around. She had been so lost in thought that she hadn't realised she was already halfway across the gardens to the drawbridge. The dewy grass made her feet itch. She had never understood how Fredryck and Vaughn had enjoyed wrestling with each other on the grass. The very thought of it made her itch all over. With a shudder, she turned her mind to the task ahead of her.

How am I going to get out of the castle without the guards seeing me?

The sandstone wall surrounding the islet was too high to climb over and the door to the drawbridge was locked and guarded at this time of night.

This is insane! What am I doing?

Kora shut down all thoughts but one. Pér would make her feel better. She so badly needed to feel better right now. She needed sleep. Sleep would not come with bloody images in her mind.

She stared up at the looming wall. There were guards stationed at the gate and at every corner. Not knowing what else to do, Kora chose a point mid-way between the gate and one corner, where the shadows fell darkest, and set to work with her power. She had never tried anything like this before but, as she had learned in the Outworld, you could never predict when you might need to use your power in unexpected ways.

Kora pulled out all her spare power. Painstakingly slowly, she pushed it to the top of the castle wall then smoothed it out towards herself before taking the first step. It was like climbing a hill – a very steep hill. She was out of breath by the time she got to the top. Afraid the guards would hear her heavy breathing, she clamped her free hand over her mouth to deaden the sound.

She sat on top of the wall, legs dangling over the moat side. In a tumbling mess, she hauled her power over the wall and down the other side, stretching it out to where the cobbled bridge began. It was a decent distance, but Kora knew she was already more powerful than most, though she had taken great pains not to show anyone the full extent of her powers. People were scared enough of Aislen's power, she didn't want them to be scared of hers as well.

Once she had caught her breath, she sat on her power and slid down to the bridge. Only halfway down did she realise she was going too fast.

Ouch!

Kora pulled the thought within her walls as the heels of her feet were shredded. She tumbled along, dropping her shoes, and ended by smacking her forehead on the cobblestones.

Stupid, stupid idea!

Kora stood up shakily and attempted to brush herself off, quickly stopping when she realised her hands were badly grazed. No longer able to even walk properly, Kora tiptoed barefoot through the streets of Illaria to Pér's house.

Now what? she thought as she stood outside his house. Her eyes strayed from the jacarandas painted on the door and up to the windows on the second storey. *I can't just knock on the door. His parents will wake up ... so might the neighbours at this time of night.*

Kora stood on the doorstep for a long moment before deciding to return to the castle. She limped a few steps along the path before she heard the door scrape open. Kora turned to see a sleepy-looking Pér smiling at her.

"Come inside," he whispered. "I'll heal you."

She had purposely come here to see Pér, to tell him how sorry she was that she had ignored him, but now she found herself hesitating. It wasn't fair of her.

Just because I feel guilty about letting him make me feel better, doesn't mean I should be angry with him over it.

"Kora, don't worry so much," he told her as he ushered her inside. Kora would have thought he was reading her mind but for the fact that she hadn't let his mind brush against hers, nor was there any skin contact.

She didn't say anything until they were up in his sparsely furnished room. Her eyes flitted around, making note of the narrow bed covered in old, patched blankets, the plain wooden chest at the end of the bed, presumably for his clothes, and a lute lying on top of it.

"You can sit here," Pér motioned to his bed. Kora looked at it uncertainly. This was starting to seem like a bad idea. It was the middle of the night. She had escaped from the castle, run through town unescorted and was now unaccompanied in a man's room.

A boy's room, she corrected herself. *He's not old enough to call him a man.*

Making a decision, she sat on the chest at the end of the bed instead. Pér made no comment on her choice.

"May I?" he asked as he knelt by her side and took her bloodied feet in his hands to heal them. In all the conversations she'd had with Pér, all the songs she'd listened to, she realised he had never actually touched her skin before. At his surprisingly warm and tender, but firm touch, Kora's skin tingled. She found she could not speak so nodded instead.

She silently watched as he healed her feet, then stopped herself from flinching as he moved his hands to her elbows, hands and head. He healed her as well as anyone under Mistress Chandrelle's tutelage could have.

She could still feel the touch of his hands against her skin, even when they had moved to a different place. Master Amyas' warning rang through her mind. She shut up her thoughts and her power behind her wall. With Pér's skin contact, he would feel and hear everything if she wasn't careful.

When he was done, Pér sat at the head of his bed, as far away from her as possible. Kora felt ridiculously injured by this.

Well, of course he'd try to get as far away from me as possible. I've been horrible to him and probably offended him. Her own thoughts were harsh. They often had been of late. Why should she be easy on herself now?

"I can't play for you at this time of night," Pér said, "but I can sing softly. I don't know if it will work as well."

She blinked, startled by his voice, and looked into his kind and accepting eyes. Kora shook her head. "I'm sorry," she said, her voice thick with tears she refused to shed. She swallowed hard and cleared her throat. "It was selfish and unfair of me to come. I'll go."

"Please ... stay." Pér held out a hand towards her as she stood. "There's nothing selfish or unfair in this. Everyone with half a brain in the castle can see you haven't been sleeping. You're always so distracted in our lessons. If I can do something to help you, then you should not feel ashamed to ask."

Ashamed, Kora thought. *That's exactly what it is! How does he know that without touching my mind?*

She had nothing left to say. They both knew why she was there. All that was left was for her to decide whether to stay or not. Kora didn't know if it should have been so easy a decision, but it was. She sat back down on the chest, still thinking it inappropriate to sit on his bed.

"May I sing to you then?" Pér asked cautiously. Kora nodded "Close your eyes."

Biting her lip, Kora closed her eyes, but pulled a few tendrils of her power out and let them float around her. She trusted so few people in her life. So many of them thought it was their right to manipulate her feelings through touch.

She could barely hear the words, but the tune carried over to her in soft, sweet hums. It took a moment before her hunched shoulders began to fall. She sucked in a deep breath and the constriction around her chest eased as she exhaled. Slowly, all the muscles that had been tense for weeks were finally starting to relax.

Chapter Five

Kora woke with a start. She'd had the strangest dream of fleeing the castle and spending the night in someone else's bed. Her eyes adjusted to the pre-dawn light. She took in her surroundings and realised it hadn't been a dream. Her cheeks flushed hotly. She was in Pér's bed. Pér was asleep on the floor, lying in front of the door.

Blocking the doorway. Kora thought slowly. *How am I going to get home before father, or the guards, realise I'm not there?*

Kora pulled back the blankets and swung her feet out of the bed. She did not remember lying down last night, let alone sliding in under the blankets. Her feet lightly touched the wooden floorboards. She wondered if anyone would find her shoes in the marketplace before she did. Kora's heart beat faster as she tiptoed around to the chest at the end of Pér's bed.

Looking again at Pér, she knew she could not get out the door without waking him. The door opened inwards. She didn't want to get him in as much trouble as she was certain to be in if anyone realised she wasn't in her own room. There was a small window on the opposite wall, barely big enough for her to crawl through, but she knew that would be her only escape.

As quietly as she could, Kora tried to lift the wooden latch that kept the window closed. It would not budge. She pressed her palm against the latch and pushed up hard. It came free with a sudden jerk. Before she could catch the latch, the window swung open and crashed against the outer wall.

"Kora!" Pér called out in surprise, his head and feet bumping against the wall. Rubbing his head, he sat up against the door. "What are you doing?"

Kora heard footsteps thumping outside the door. The door handle rattled.

"Pér, are you all right?"

"I'm fine," he replied loudly. "I just fell out of bed."

"Not again," came the mumbled reply from the other side of the door. Kora frowned at Pér curiously. He put his fingers to his lips and she stayed silent, hands poised to drag herself out of the window.

The footsteps receded, and Kora pulled her hands away from the window, suddenly feeling quite silly for her ridiculous escape strategy.

"Walk down beside me. They won't notice your footsteps then," he whispered. "I'll say I need to go to the library early today and walk you back you back to the castle."

Kora wanted to protest that she didn't need an escort, but it made her feel oddly special that he wanted to do that for her. Instead, she nodded and wrapped her power snugly around herself, blending into the background.

Pér walked down the stairs slowly, and Kora walked impatiently by his side. She didn't want to stay in the house any longer than necessary. When Pér went to talk to his parents, Kora stayed back in the shadows near the front door. As soon as Pér opened it, she fled out into the street, staying close to the shadows. She knew he was expecting her to stay by his side, but she didn't have time. Dawn had already tinged the sky orange. The guards would soon be lowering the drawbridge and the castle servants would be going about their work. If she wasn't at least in the castle by the time anyone came looking for her, it would be suspicious.

My shoes! I'll need to find them too.

As she made it back to the hallways to her room, she could see her sister knocking on the door. Kora ducked back around the corner, put her shoes on and pulled her power back within her wall. Completely visible again, she walked casually around the corner.

"You're going to wake half the castle" she snapped. "What do you want?"

"What do I want?" Nyssa cried out, incredulous and shrill. "You've been avoiding me since we got back home. You can't just abandon me!"

"Abandon you?" Kora laughed bitterly. "I think you've been just fine, surrounded by everyone else. You don't need *me* too."

Nyssa faltered. Kora saw the crushed look in her eyes and felt the slightest twinge of guilt.

"I *do* need you, Kora," Nyssa said in a much softer voice. "You're my *sister* – the only one I have left. It feels like you've disappeared too, even though you're right here. I ... I miss you."

Kora took a tentative step forward and reached her arm out towards her sister. The spark of love and hope in Nyssa's eyes wounded her even more than the crushed look had felt a moment earlier. Kora held her thoughts and feelings tightly behind her wall before she reached out properly to hug her sister. If Nyssa was aware of the precaution Kora took, she didn't say anything. Kora was relieved. It was not the time to bicker over their differences of opinion when it came to the use of their power.

Chapter Six

Pér avoided her gaze and crossed his arms when she walked into the healing lesson that afternoon with Nyssa. She knew why, but it still made her blush with embarrassment. It had been wrong of her to leave him stranded in the street, and not meet him in the library where she knew he would be that morning.

"You didn't wait for me," Pér stated the obvious as she stood beside him.

"I know," Kora replied.

There was an awkward silence between them. Kora felt like kicking herself for her behaviour but found she couldn't bring herself to apologise.

Mistress Chandrelle walked into the room after the last student and closed the door firmly behind her. She looked around the class. Kora felt the healing mistress' eyes linger on her a moment longer than necessary.

"I'm glad to see you've finally gotten some rest, Kora. Tired students make dangerous mistakes in my class. I will not allow anyone to knowingly place another lintep in danger."

Kora bit back a sullen retort. She knew, better than anyone in their class, how dangerous healing could be.

"New partners today," Mistress Chandrelle addressed the class. "I don't want to see anyone with a partner they've had before."

Kora looked at the other students, who began pairing off. Soon, there were only a handful left. Her stomach lurched when she realised the only one she hadn't worked with before was Lishe.

Lishe was a few years older than her and had started lessons in the castle the same year as Nyssa. From all accounts, she was very talented and worked hard at all her lessons. But there was something about her that sat badly with Kora. She couldn't put her finger on it, but Kora was glad that Lishe had so little power. There was a limit to what she would ever be capable of. It was the only reason Kora wasn't frightened of her.

"Kora," Lishe said with a satisfied smile, "I've been waiting months to work with you. I can't wait to see if you are as powerful as your big sister."

"Not everything is about power, Lishe," Kora answered shortly.

"True," Lishe replied with a wave of her hand. "Power isn't everything, but it certainly helps when you don't bother to hone your skills, like some."

Kora followed Lishe's gaze to Nyssa. It was no secret to any of their classmates that Nyssa did as little practise as possible outside of their classes and only ever did enough in her classes to pass to the next stage. Nyssa should have been in a more advanced class than Kora, but because Kora paid more attention and worked harder at her lessons, they shared many classes. Unfortunately, Lishe was in most of those classes as well. Kora had avoided working with her until now.

Mistress Chandrelle clapped her hands together loudly. "To your seats please."

Kora followed Lishe to the workstation furthest from Mistress Chandrelle's desk. There was a small knife and a lantern on each of the workstations. She began to get a very uneasy feeling about this lesson.

"Depending on your courage, you may work with either small incisions or minor burns today. I will be observing and assessing each of you to ensure everyone is working safely and well within their limits."

Kora sat across from Lishe and picked up the knife. Some lintep wanted to injure their own subjects before healing them. Kora was not going to give Lishe that chance. She nicked one of her fingertips with the blade and offered her hand to Lishe.

Lishe gave her a look of disappointment. "Is that all?"

"We've never worked with each other before," Kora said with a shrug. "I want to start small."

"Are you sure you aren't just scared of what happened to your family?"

Kora gasped in surprise. Had Lishe really said that?

"Just heal me and be done with it." Kora held out her hand. She didn't want Lishe touching her, but there was no other way – healing involved touch. The older girl's fingers were cold, bony and not at all gentle.

Kora was very careful to keep all her thoughts to herself. She did not want the contrast between *this* healing and the healing last night to become food for gossip.

"Oh Nyssa!" Mistress Chandrelle cried out in dismay. "You really need to practise more. How do you ever expect to perfect even the simplest tasks in my class unless you take the time to hone your skills?"

As Lishe healed her fingertip, Kora glanced over at Nyssa. Her sister's face was bright red in embarrassment. Both Nyssa and her partner had bloody fingers. Kora sighed. She didn't even have to guess what had happened. Nyssa had clearly lost her focus and opened a matching wound in her own hand without healing her partner's. It was a beginner mistake. One that Nyssa had stopped making months ago. But ...

Mother had known better than that as well, before she killed herself trying to save Vaughn.

Kora turned back to Lishe when the black-haired girl roughly tossed her healed hand aside. Lishe picked up the lantern, frowned in concentration and lit it.

"Do you want to burn me – or should I do it myself?" she asked, clearly expecting Kora to shy away from the task.

Kora ground her teeth together. If it had been anyone else, she *would* have let them do it themselves. But then again, no one else in their class would have suggested she burn them in the first place.

"I'll do it."

Kora took the lantern from Lishe and placed it on the table between them. Then she took Lishe's hand firmly in her own and pressed it against the metal of the lantern for three heartbeats.

Lishe didn't so much as flinch. Kora suppressed a shudder as she turned Lishe's hand over to examine the red and swollen skin. She took a steadying breath and closed her eyes, holding both of Lishe's hands in her own. She studied the difference between them with her power, then set to work. She did nothing so kind as to take the pain away from Lishe – if the girl was stupid enough to choose the flame over the knife, then she could live with the pain.

Kora stopped what she was doing and looked at Lishe's hands. The swelling had gone down and the skin was almost back to its normal shade.

She suppressed a smile of satisfaction, but internally glowed with pride. Mistress Chandrelle had only recently mentioned that she might be allowed to move up to the advanced class. Kora was eager to show Mistress Chandrelle that she would not be mistaken in elevating her when she was still so young. Nyssa and Lishe should already have been there, along with most of their friends, but Nyssa rarely took the time to practice and Lishe did not have enough power to do as much as would be required in the more advanced classes.

Lishe's bony fingers grabbed her by the wrist and forced her hand towards the lantern. Kora struggled against the grip in a panic.

"What are you doing?" she hissed at Lishe.

Her partner raised an eyebrow at her. "You think you get to burn me and I won't return the favour? Now stop squirming or I might *accidentally* burn you more than I intend to."

Kora's eyes widened in terror.

"Let me go," she whispered, her voice trembling. "I never agreed to that."

"You owe me one time," Lishe replied unflinchingly. "It's your choice what happens after that."

Kora tried to draw her hand back but Lishe only tugged harder and pushed Kora's hand firmly onto the lantern. Kora screamed as her flesh bubbled and blistered. By the time Lishe let her hand go, some of the blisters had popped open and were weeping.

"Oops, sorry." Lishe put a hand over her mouth in mock shock, but Kora could see the smile behind it.

"Lishe! That was very irresponsible. Fix her hand *now*," Mistress Chandrelle ordered as she came over to watch.

Through her pain and horror, Kora realised this had been Lishe's plan all along. It was the only way anyone would allow her to attempt to heal such a major wound and force Mistress Chandrelle to consider her for the advanced class.

"Yes, Mistress Chandrelle," Lishe replied in a subdued voice.

Kora would have slapped her but for the fact that she was holding her mutilated hand at the wrist with her good hand. She had learned, some time ago, that if she surrounded the injured part of her body with her power, it effectively cut off the feeling of pain. It was the only way she had ever made it through her first healing tests. But Lishe had caught her by surprise and she hadn't had the chance to do it.

Lishe worked painfully slowly, under the watchful eye of Mistress Chandrelle. Kora watched with morbid interest. She had never healed as bad a burn as this before and wanted to see what Lishe would do and if Mistress Chandrelle would correct her at all.

By the time Lishe was done, the entire class had crowded around them. Mistress Chandrelle shooed them away with a wave of her hand.

"That was quite well done, Lishe, though I do not understand how the two of you were so clumsy as to create such a burn in the first place. Please be more careful in the future."

"Yes, Mistress Chandrelle," Kora mumbled and heard Lishe echo her in a sickly-sweet voice.

Relief flooded through Kora as she heard the bell toll for the end of lessons. Without a word to anyone, Kora fled the room, ran straight to her chambers and locked the door behind her.

Chapter Seven

The healing lesson had ripped open the wounds Kora had been trying so hard to heal since she had returned from the Outworld. The sight of Nyssa making the same mistake both Vaughn and their mother had made had completely undone her. It hadn't helped that Lishe had taken advantage in that moment of weakness. She never wanted to work with her again. How could Nyssa call her a friend?

"She's not so bad," Nyssa replied with a shrug when Kora asked her. "She said she'd help me practise outside of class. No one else has ever offered to."

Kora couldn't believe her ears. "Perhaps that's because you haven't expressed the slightest interest in practising outside of class! I'm sure there would be plenty of people willing to work with you. Why *Lishe*?"

Nyssa shrugged. "She doesn't have much power, so I'll always be able to do more than her."

"Really?" Kora asked in shock. "*That's* the reason? You shouldn't be comparing yourself with someone who has as little power as Lishe. You should be practicing with Daegan and Braedan instead. Neither of them could surpass your power, but at least they more closely match it."

Nyssa shot Kora a look she couldn't read. "I've never gotten along that well with Daegan, and Braedan ... we were closer when we were younger. Not so much now."

"What's wrong with Braedan?" Kora asked in bafflement.

Nyssa gave her an exasperated look. "Nothing."

"Tell me," Kora pleaded. Nyssa shook her head. "I remember you being best friends when you were little. *You* were the one who convinced him that humans aren't as bad as Uncle Kynon thinks they are."

Kora didn't realise what she'd said until it was too late. Humans had killed more than half their family. Nyssa stared at her coldly.

"If you must know, Braedan stopped talking to me so much once you joined our lessons."

"What?" Kora took a step back. "That's not true."

Nyssa shook her head again. "I didn't want to tell you. But it's true. Braedan likes you better than he likes me, so ... I don't think we'd work together very well anymore."

Kora didn't try to stop her when Nyssa left her chambers. She was in too much shock to react.

Kora couldn't sleep. Again. She tossed and turned in her bed. It was too hot under the covers, but she froze without them. If only the temperature was her problem. She was plagued by guilty thoughts. She could barely breathe, they crushed her so. Knowing it was pointless trying to sleep, she hopped out of bed, dressed warmly and walked down to the library. Guiscard rarely kept it open so late, but she could think of nowhere else to go.

The library door was locked. Kora trusted neither her skill at lock-picking nor her luck to hold out enough for her to enter alone without anyone finding out.

Now what? she thought to herself. *Everyone is asleep but me.*

She walked the halls aimlessly, not willing to go back to her own chambers.

"Kora?" Aislen's voice called out softly. Kora blinked and looked around. She was surprised to notice she was on the top floor of the castle. Aislen's head was poked around her bedroom door. "Come in here."

Curious, Kora stepped into her cousin's room. Aislen was a good deal older than her, but that had never got in the way of their relationship. She had always been one of Kora's favourite people. Perhaps it was because she was one of the few who understood how Kora felt about how lintep used their powers without any regard for anyone else.

"Can't sleep?" Aislen asked as she offered Kora a cup of tea. Kora sat beside her on the chaise and took the cup with a grateful smile but froze as she breathed in the scent. It was the same lavender tea her mother used to make for her when she couldn't sleep. Kora put the cup down on the low table in front of her and walked away to the other side of the room.

"It will get better," Aislen patted the seat next to her on the long chaise. "I know it doesn't feel like it now, but you'll learn to live without them. One day, you'll be happy for the things that remind you of them."

"Not today," Kora said, wrapping her arms around herself as she stood alone. She did not sit next to Aislen.

"Not today," Aislen conceded. She rose gracefully and walked over to Kora. Aislen embraced her, not letting her skin touch Kora's. The pressure all around her somehow relaxed Kora. She unclenched her hands from her arms and flung them around Aislen, hugging her tightly. Kora felt Aislen loosen her hold ever so slightly and pulled in her closer, not willing to let go just yet. Aislen did not object but stayed in the embrace for as long as Kora needed.

Eventually, Kora let go. She wiped the tears from her eyes, not remembering crying.

"Try the tea," Aislen told her. "It might remind you of Aunt Graesyn, but it will still help you sleep."

She held the cup in her hands for a moment before offering it to Kora. There was steam rising off the liquid once again. Kora smiled at the easy and homely way Aislen used her power to warm a tepid cup of tea. She reached out for the cup and took a deep breath, smelling the lavender once more. This time, it was not too much to bear. She drank the tea slowly. Aislen disappeared into her bed chamber and soon returned with a blanket.

"Lie down here tonight. It doesn't matter if you sleep or not, but you'll know that I'm just in the next room if you need me."

Kora nodded gratefully and held out the now empty cup as she took the blanket from Aislen. Trying not to think of anything, she pulled the blanket up to her chin as she lay down on the chaise.

Chapter Eight

Kora sat up sleepily. She had drifted off into a fitful doze sometime during the night. Nightmares kept startling her awake, taking away her ability to rest. The grey sky showed it was still early morning when she finally decided there was no point lying down anymore.

She folded the blanket and left it on the chaise before tiptoeing out of Aislen's chambers. She didn't bother going back to her own chambers – there was nothing she needed from there. It only took her a moment to remember that there were no classes today. The teachers got two days off each week from their duties. Students and teachers who boarded in the castle often used that time to visit their families in the city or out on the farmlands. They would have left the night before, to make the most of their time off. It meant the castle would be quieter than usual today.

Kora walked past the library, grinding her teeth at the closed door. Guiscard would certainly open it today, but clearly not until later. Her stomach rumbled, and she almost doubled over in pain.

Food, she reminded herself, *food is just as important as sleep.*

She hadn't eaten since the horrifying healing class. It was too early for the dining hall to be serviced, but Kora knew the kitchen staff would already be hard at work. Perhaps she could pilfer a bread roll.

The homely aroma of freshly baked bread wafted over to her as she neared the kitchen on the lowest level of the castle. There would be another entrance to them somewhere, but she only knew the location of the one from the dining hall. Her footsteps echoed as she walked along the sandstone floor.

She opened the kitchen door with a heavy-shouldered shove. She often wondered how the kitchen staff could open it so easily with heavily laden trays of food.

No one looked up as she entered. They were all too focused on their tasks. A few heads turned as she walked among them, but quickly looked back to their workstations when they realised who she was. From a young age, she had walked through the kitchens unaccompanied. Most of the staff dismissed her presence out of hand, as she did not bother any of them. On occasion, she received a grumbled reprimand, but they never actually stopped her from taking any food she wanted.

As unobtrusively as possible, she walked over to the cooling racks full of small bread rolls. They were still steaming hot. She took one in each hand and shoved them into her skirt pockets. The heat of the rolls burned through to her legs, forcing her to hold her skirt out at arm's length on each side. It made her far more noticeable as she walked towards the baskets of fruit.

"Are you planning a feast for yourself?" a kitchen hand called out to her in a snide voice.

Kora stared at the girl in shock. Only the cooks generally admonished her and, even then, they were at least polite.

"I don't see that it's any of your business," Kora replied harshly.

The kitchenhand stopped what she was doing and placed her hands on her hips, staring coldly at Kora.

"We're the ones slaving away in the kitchen getting food ready for the entire castle and you think you can just waltz in here to take whatever you like?"

Kora was saved the embarrassment of replying by Cook Tobias, who walked up from behind and placed a hand on her shoulder.

"Yasmina, show a little respect for Lady Kora," Cook Tobias reprimanded the furious girl. "If you had bothered to notice, she neither dined in the hall last night, nor called for food to be brought to her room. Hunger must be eating away at her by now. Would you deny her the two rolls she would have eaten for breakfast anyway?"

Yasmina turned pale at the mention of Kora's name. It hadn't occurred to Kora that the kitchen hands may not recognise her by sight. Had she been a student in the castle, she likely would never have dared walk so brazenly through the kitchen. But what surprised her the most was that Cook Tobias had noticed her lack of appetite.

"Apologies, Lady Kora," Yasmina said with an awkward curtsey. "Would you like some strawberry jam to go along with your bread?"

Kora's anger quickly subsided, but not completely. "No, thank you. I was just going to get an apple before getting out of your way."

Yasmina stepped out of the way of the fruit baskets. Kora looked up at Cook Tobias with a short smile. He lifted his hand from her shoulder and gestured towards the fruit. Kora took a pale green apple from the top of the basket and turned to leave. When she realised Cook Tobias was following her, she slowed to let him catch up.

"My lady, I hope you don't mind, but I took the liberty of sending food up for Lord Aaron when I realised no one had rung for him."

Kora looked up at him in anguish. That was her task. *She* was the one who had been calling down for his food. Wrapped in her own grief, she had forgotten to take care of him.

"I …" She didn't know what to say.

Cook Tobias shook his head.

"It's not right for such a young daughter to have to look after her father," he told her gently. "Please, do not trouble yourself. I will arrange that food be sent up to him three times a day if he is not seen in the eating hall. Will that be satisfactory?"

Kora raised a hand to cover her mouth, trying to hide her trembling lips, and nodded.

"Very well then, it is settled." He breathed deeply, as though a weight had been lifted off his shoulders. "If you will permit me, you must look after yourself as well as you do your father. You are well loved, Lady Kora. Allow your friends and your family to look be there for you.

"As for my kitchen, the doors are always open to you. Even if you only have need of some tea leaves, we will find something to calm your nerves. Yasmina will never dare to speak so boldly and cruelly to you again."

Kora was so overwhelmed by his kindness, she threw her arms around his neck and held him tightly. After a moment's stiff surprise, the old cook relaxed and returned her hug, patting her softly on the back.

Chapter Nine

As Kora walked to the courtyard, she thought about what Cook Tobias had said. It was true, she had purposely been keeping almost everyone at arm's length since she returned. She hadn't even considered why. Maybe she didn't want anyone else to get close to her. It wasn't that she thought everyone she was close to would die. That wasn't it at all. But the pain of losing *so* many people in her family had burnt a hole in her heart, and it felt like that hole would only get bigger with every death or loss she would face the rest of her life. If she just kept to herself, maybe the hole wouldn't ever burn through her whole heart and she might just be able to survive.

It made a twisted sort of sense. But she could also see why Cook Tobias thought she was making a mistake. His kindness, and Aislen's the night before, had warmed her, had made her actually *feel* something through the numbness that usually surrounded her.

Kora sat on one of the sandstone ledges edging the inner courtyard. It was deserted at this time of morning. She loved the solitude – it allowed her to freely practice her skills without fear of reprimand or ridicule. Carefully wrapping the apple with her power, she allowed it to hover in front of her eyes. With practiced ease, she sent it on a journey around the perimeter of the courtyard. Once satisfied that she had focussed enough attention on it, she pulled one of the bread rolls out of her skirt pocket. She tore bits off and popped them into her mouth while performing different manoeuvres with the apple.

It was a calming process. Once she had settled on a course for the apple, she closed her eyes to see if she could manage it without bumping it into any walls. If she failed, she would be rewarded with a bruised apple to finish her early breakfast.

By the time she had finished eating both bread rolls, Kora was bored of moving her apple around the courtyard, in and out of the sandstone arches. She titled her head to look up at the clear blue sky. The lack of cloud cover was certainly helping to warm the day, but after the chilly night, the sun had a lot of work to do. She idly wondered how up into that clear sky she would be able to push her apple if she tried.

Her practical masters had often tried to gauge the limit of her powers, without success. Her power had started to peak earlier in the season, but Kora knew it was still increasing. Her father had made her train all her life so that her peaking power would never be a problem. She had noticed random surges but, with practise, it took less than a few hours for her to realign how much power she needed for particular tasks.

Since her trip to the Outworld, Master Elwood, who was her current practical teacher, had not tested her limits. Perhaps he thought she was too unsettled to try. Kora frowned. If he wouldn't test her, she would test herself.

The apple shot up into the sky. Kora watched as it grew smaller and smaller, until it disappeared completely. She sighed, angry that she couldn't determine the strength of her power by herself and pulled it back down. Blinded by irritation, she lost her focus. The apple smashed to pieces in the middle of the pathways intersecting the courtyard. It hit with such force that some of the apple splattered her skirt, and she slipped off her perch in surprise.

"I'm glad it's not just me you're treating badly."

There was a hint of mockery in his voice, and Kora cringed as she looked up into Pér's face from where she was sprawled on the ground. He offered her a hand, but she refused it. She had no right to be angry with him but, in her mind, if she couldn't accept his unique way of helping her cope, she had to refuse his help with something as simple as standing.

Pér awkwardly kept his hand out as she got to her feet then tucked it into his jacket pocket. She looked away from him to dust the stray pieces of apple from her skirt.

"Why didn't you come over last night?" he asked, frowning.

Kora's hands stopped half way down her skirt, and she stared at him.

"What?" she asked incredulously. "How could you possibly expect me come after you got so angry with me last time?"

Pér's laughter rumbled out of him and echoed around the courtyard. "That's *not* what I was angry about," he told her, when he finished laughing. "I was angry that you didn't walk with me to the castle like you said you would. You just left without saying anything and barely spoke to me, even in our lessons."

"But ... what?" Kora shook her head in disbelief. "I thought ..."

"Kora, I have a unique gift. We both know that. Why would I ever deny the comfort that gift can bring to you?" His voice was soft, gentle.

Kora didn't realise how close he was to her until their lips were almost touching. Her heart stopped for a second, then started racing furiously. Her cheeks burned with a deep blush. He stayed there, waiting. It was her decision. He was making that painfully obvious.

Trying not to think – not daring to think – she leaned forward ever so slightly and let her lips brush over his. A sigh escaped on his breath. Kora couldn't help but smile as she pulled away from him, her cheeks and now her lips burning.

She laughed as Pér nearly lost his balance leaning in towards her and held him up with a hand on his chest. He stumbled forward a step and clasped his hand over hers. His walls were down – purposely down. All his thoughts, hopes, dreams of her were there for her to see. One glimpse was enough. She tore her hand away from his and ran.

Kora did not stop running until she had reached the library. It was finally open. Without bothering to greet Guiscard, though she glimpsed a smile on his face as she ran through the doors, she hurried to the furthest, darkest corner of the library she could find. Sitting on the floor, her knees pulled up tightly to her chest, she dragged her trailing power back behind her wall. Pér's appearance had surprised her so much that she had not realised how much of her power was still floating around outside her body.

Was that why he had bared himself to her? Had he seen more of her than she intended anyone to see? Did he feel obliged to show her because she had unwittingly shown him something?

What she had seen in that one glimpse terrified her. A future for the two of them – a happy one. This kiss, this one stupid kiss, meant so much to him. It meant so much to her as well – too much – but she didn't want another person to mourn if things went badly. It would hurt too much. It would burn that hole to the very edges of her heart. She couldn't do it. Kora buried her head in her arms and wept bitterly.

Chapter Ten

"Kora?"

Kora looked up as her father walked down the dark aisle towards her. She was leafing through the pages of an old book, but closed it as he approached, and placed it on the shelf beside her.

"I've been looking for you all morning," he told her. "The kitchen maid who brought my food made it clear that you did not order my food last night or this morning."

Kora didn't reply. What could she possibly say?

"I'm sorry, Kora." He took her hands in his. Kora flinched away until she realised his power was withdrawn. His face fell, and he dropped her hands. She instantly regretted her lack of trust in him. "I only wanted to thank you. I know I've been absent. I know you've taken too much on yourself. I know."

Kora shook her head. "What else could I have done?" She wasn't angry with him. Not at first. But as she thought of every task that had fallen to her since their return because he was not willing or capable enough to do it himself, her anger intensified.

"You could have let someone else take care of me." He took a step back, as though her anger was a force radiating out of her. Perhaps it was. She checked her power and realised it was floating all around her, protecting her. Frustrated, she pulled it back inside her walls.

"Your teachers tell me your power is increasing every day," he said. "I only wanted to tell you I'm still here for you. If you want to practise with me, pick my brains or ... even argue with me ... I'm here."

"You don't want to argue with me, father," she said quietly. "My qualms about how lintep in Illaria use their power is still the same as ever."

She paused when she saw the shock on his face.

"Even after what happened to mother, Vaughn, Fredryck and Adina," she spoke firmly. "There were many humans in Hedgefall who did *not* wish us any harm. I do not think that humans, in general, are the problem. There are enough lintep, just in my classes, that I don't like, but I don't think our entire race is like that."

Her father said nothing for long moments. She could see him warring with himself, with his differing opinions.

"I respect your ideas," he told her through gritted teeth. "But I will never again put my trust in humans. If I fear my family is in danger, I will plough through their thoughts until I am satisfied they mean no harm. If I find it necessary to change their mood, I will not hesitate to do that, to even an entire mob of them.

"However, if *you* wish not to and you insist that no lintep should use those powers on you, I will do my best to ensure it. I will discuss the matter with your teachers. If they agree that it is the wisest course of action, they too will refrain from manipulating your feelings or reading your thoughts."

Kora knew it would be asking too much for him to change his views, but she was overwhelmingly grateful that he understood how much her own views meant to her.

"Thank you, father." She stepped forward, took his hands in her and kissed his fingertips. It was what he used to do when she was a child and it had always made her smile. With a tearful smile, her father kissed her fingertips in return.

Kora spent the rest of the day holed up in the library. In that dark aisle, where she'd initially closeted herself, she'd found some interesting things to read. There were old parchments and books with yellowing pages, all on lintep interactions with humans and, in more recent texts, the war. The earlier parchments had no mention of lintep using their powers on humans in so blatant and unfair a fashion as had later become commonplace. It gave Kora hope that things might one day return to that state.

She read differing accounts of the war Princess Rilla had died in. The main point of contention was *when* she had actually died. Kora knew that most lintep were under the misconception that she had been killed by humans in the heat of battle, but her family knew otherwise. Princess Rilla had been something of a taboo topic when Kora was younger. She had always been too afraid to ask anything about her but had listened intently whenever her name was mentioned.

At one point, late in the afternoon, Guiscard approached her. "Kora, dear, you haven't left the library all day. I must insist you join your friends in the eating hall or your family in their chambers."

The mention of food made her stomach rumble, killing off the protest that was on the tip of her tongue. Kora looked between Guiscard and the books and parchments sprawled out in front of her.

"The parchments, no. The books – give them to me and I'll see which I can allow you to borrow."

Kora closed the books and laid them in the librarian's arms. He carried the hefty pile of books to the front of the library, leaving Kora to clear away the mess of parchments. She climbed the ladder and replaced them in their rightful places. As she did so, her fingers brushed against a small book. Kora took another step up to the top rung and reached higher until she could wrap her hand around it.

She pulled it out and stepped down a few rungs as she regained her balance. Kora turned the book over in her hand, looking at the brown leather covering the front, back and spine. There was no gold lettering as with the other books she had leafed through. Nothing to distinguish it as anything of importance. But if it was here, she reasoned it must have something to do with the same time period.

When she handed the book to Guiscard, he looked at it curiously, turned it over and examined it in more detail than she herself had. He shrugged and handed it back to her.

"I'll mark it down as nameless, but that does not mean you can keep it. Is that understood?" he asked as he waggled a warning finger at her.

Kora nodded and placed the book on top of the pile Guiscard was allowing her to borrow. She smiled at the thought that at least she would have something to do of an evening when she couldn't sleep. Going to Pér's house was no longer an option.

Before he let her go, Guiscard caught her by the sleeve. "I have eyes in this castle, young lady. I will know if you do not dine with anyone tonight. If I hear that is the case, I will confiscate your books and not allow you back into the library until I am satisfied you are not becoming a hermit. Is that clear?"

"Not *all* of the books in my chambers are yours, Guiscard," Kora replied irritably.

Guiscard gave her a hard stare. "That's as may be, but I know you must have read those books a hundred times each or you wouldn't be in here every other day finding new things to read. Don't test me on this, Kora. I know where your weaknesses lie."

Kora huffed and took the books away without another word. If she hadn't been convinced that he would carry out his threat, Kora would have stayed in her chambers that evening, and all the next day. As it was, she left the books on her desk, locked the door behind herself and walked down to the dining hall. She did not want to talk to her father again. Not after that morning.

Chapter Eleven

The dining hall was rather subdued as Kora filled a plate. Luisella had gone home for the two-day break, so Braedan was dining with his twin brother, Daegan, instead. Nyssa and Lishe were sitting across the hall from them, talking quietly. There were a handful of other students and teachers who had decided not to go home for the break. Then, there was Pér. He was sitting at the hearth, strumming his lute and singing a melancholy song.

She wondered if anyone else understood that their mood was subdued because of his melody. She remembered when she had first understood that his gift was unique and powerful.

It had been one day in the marketplace – at least five years ago. Pér's family sold fabrics, fine enough for the people who lived in the city itself, but durable enough to allow them to carry out their day's work without fear of ruining their clothes. Kora and her father had been walking through the marketplace on their way to buy the cinnamon scrolls she loved the best. A small child ran in front of them, making her father stumble. Kora caught and steadied him, but in the commotion, the child fell and scraped her knee on the cobblestones.

Pér had run over to them. He had only just started coming to the castle for lessons, so Kora had barely known him. She had watched as he helped the girl to her feet, led her over to his family's stall and popped her up on a wooden stool. The little girl's dirt-smudged face had rivulets of tears streaming down it.

She'd observed with interest as Pér pulled out a lute from behind the stall and began to play it for the child. A small smile had crept over the girl's face and her tears dried up. Kora remembered tugging her father over to heal the girl's knees. As they'd drawn closer, the melody from the lute had washed over her. She'd felt happy and hopeful for the day ahead, without any particular thing to look forward to. Her eyes had widened in surprise as she realised it was the music making her feel that way.

To test her theory, she'd left her father with Pér and the girl and run towards the bakery. When she could no longer hear the music, her jubilant feelings had been quite quickly subdued. She'd bought four scrolls – two cinnamon, two apple.

As she again approached the fabric stall, Pér's music reached out to her, pulling her in closer. She'd felt safe and comfortable. It was such a pleasant sensation, so unlike when her parents or teachers had tried to force her mood to change through touch. This had felt so natural, so ... nice.

Kora handed the scrolls to her father, Pér and the little girl. When the music stopped, the feelings lessened, but did not entirely disappear. Pér had winked at her puzzled smile.

It was only once Pér had become confident enough to play in the eating hall in the castle that Kora had mentioned her discovery to her father. He had doubted her at first, but she eventually dragged him down to the eating hall to listen to the songs one blustery evening. Even with the hearth and lanterns lit around the hall, it was usually a dismal place during storms. Pér's music had changed that. People were sitting close to one another, talking animatedly. None of them noticed the inclement weather.

Her father had taken himself and Kora over to Pér's house after that night. Pér's parents had been overwhelmed by their presence – a Lord in their house! – but her father had shrugged off their awe with the excuse of wanting to get to know one of his daughter's friends. It was the first time she had heard her father blatantly lie – she and Pér had hardly been acquaintances at the time. After talking with Pér's parents for a while, her father had asked Pér to favour them with a song.

Pér had looked towards her for assurance. She'd smiled and nodded. Apparently, that was all he needed to pull out his lute. He played a regular song, and it had no effect.

"Play for me the way you played for that little girl in the marketplace," her father said.

Pér's eyes had widened in surprise, but he'd dutifully strummed the strings of his lute, allowing a sense of comfort to wash over them. It was clumsy, and forced, but it still worked.

"Has anyone else noticed how you play?" her father had asked him. Pér had shaken his head. "Hmm, best keep it that way if you don't want to be forced into a life of service, though I can't deny you would be of great value to Lukys."

Pér's eyes bulged while Kora had covered her mouth, trying to suppress a laugh.

From that day forward, her father had taken a great interest in Pér and his unique ability. They had spent weeks together, honing his skills, finding a way to make Lukys dismiss the would-be minstrel out of hand.

"Is this your doing?" Braedan asked, snapping her out of her memory. "He's been moody all day."

"So what if it is?" Kora asked, sitting down beside Daegan and placing her full plate on the table.

"So what if it is?" Braedan repeated to Daegan with a tone of disbelief. "Kora, he's been playing all the saddest songs he can dredge up most of the day. He refuses to go outside, he refuses to eat. He won't even change the tune for a request. What did you do to him?"

"Nothing," Kora replied tersely, spearing a roast potato with her fork. "It was *his* fault anyway, not *mine*."

"So something *did* happen?" Daegan asked from beside her, more gently than his twin brother.

Kora shoved the potato into her mouth and glared at Daegan. She didn't generally have much to do with him, but he was certainly easier to talk to than Braedan. He didn't jibe her over things she was clearly uncomfortable talking about. Braedan seemed to delight in getting the worst reaction out of her possible.

"Braedan, why don't you go talk to Nyssa for a while," Daegan suggested. "You've barely spoken since she returned."

Braedan got up with an exaggerated sigh and walked across the dining hall to join Nyssa and Lishe. Kora saw the surprised expressions on the girls' faces as he sat down without so much as a greeting.

"What happened, Kora?" Daegan asked quietly.

Kora attempted to stab some peas that were being recalcitrant and rolling out from under her fork. She threw the utensil down in frustration.

"We kissed," she told him between clenched teeth.

"Did he force you to?" he asked, suddenly defensive.

Kora shook her head. "No. The kiss wasn't the problem. It's what he did after the kiss."

Daegan said nothing but took Kora's hand. She flinched away, but his grip was firm, making sure she understood that his power was withdrawn as far from her as possible.

"You see," she said looking down at their hands, "you're keeping your thoughts to yourself, and so am I. Why couldn't he just do that? Why did he have to touch my hand at all?"

Daegan squeezed her hand comfortingly. "Did it really come as a surprise to you to find out how deeply he cares for you? We've all known since the first time we met him."

"I knew he liked me, but ... you didn't see what he showed me. I can't give him that. I can't be everything he wants. I just ... can't."

Daegan looked at her thoughtfully and released her hand. "I don't think you realise, you already *are* everything he wants. He would do anything for you, anything to be in your life. He doesn't care what."

"He *should* care," Kora replied irrationally. "Why doesn't he care?"

Kora noticed the sudden silence. Pér had stopped playing and was looking straight at her. Kora panicked and checked that her power was completely withdrawn. She clutched at Daegan's arm as he rose to join his brother, but he easily evaded her.

She looked around for some way to avoid Pér. He was walking with a determined stride towards her. Without running out of the hall and causing a huge scene, there was no way to escape.

"You keep leaving me." His voice didn't have the reproachful tone she'd expected. He sat across from her, at least allowing her a breath of distance from him. "You know I'll keep finding you again."

"Not if I go far enough away," Kora replied before she could stop herself. There was a flicker of doubt in Pér's eyes.

"Tell me something, Kora. Why did you kiss me? I didn't force you to."

Kora's stomach churned as her lips burned in memory of the brief kiss, her power swirling around to fade her into the sandstone wall behind her.

"I can still feel you, even if you disappear," Pér said with a hint of amusement. "Everything about you radiates. I don't know how no one else seems to notice."

"That's why I kissed you," Kora whispered as she withdrew her power back into her mind. "You always see me. You notice everything about me. And you don't care how disappointing anyone else finds me."

"Disappointing?" Pér asked in confusion. "Who could *ever* find you a disappointment? You have strong morals and you act on them. You don't let anyone sway you into an action you think is wrong. You have a wonderful sense of humour when you aren't too sad to use it. And you ... see me. Even my parents don't understand what I do with my music."

Kora felt a smile spread across her face. She looked up into Pér's brown eyes. They looked so peaceful, so full of love. It was everything she wanted but was so afraid to accept.

"Would you like to take a turn around the gardens?" she asked shyly. Pér immediately stood and held out his arm to her. Kora rose with a little more decorum and linked her arm through his, resting her hand lightly on top of his arm. Together they walked out of the dining hall. She didn't look back to see what her sister or the twins thought of her actions.

Chapter Twelve

The nights fell into a steady rhythm. Kora would wait until the sun had gone down enough to mask her shadow as she walked, invisibly, across the courtyard to the castle wall. After her first attempt with a ramp, where she had injured herself, she had experimented. It took her a few nights to realise she could create stairs with her power – the main difficulty was trusting that she was stepping in the right place and would not fall off them.

When she trusted herself, it became much easier. Sometimes she ran through the halls with shoes in her hands, other times, she created steps from her window down to the courtyard.

Once on the other side of the moat, she would run barefoot through the cobbled streets to Pér's house. He knew to wait up for her now. As soon as he felt her presence, he would open his window for her. She had mastered the art of crawling in through his window from her invisible stairs without crashing into the furniture in his room.

It was the most peaceful part of her day, every day. He would sing her to sleep in a way that no other lintep could. Her grief did not disappear but, with Pér's help, the intensity of it lessened. Some nights, she thought she would be able to fall asleep without his help, but she kept going to him.

The seasons eased from autumn to winter until Kora looked out her window one night to see snow covering the castle gardens.

Shoes tonight, she thought to herself. She padded carefully through the castle halls, keeping to the carpeted sections to mask her footsteps. It was only when she reached the bare stairs that she thought her footsteps might be heard if anyone was nearby. She took off her shoes and practically flew down the twisted stairways to the ground level. By the time she reached the bottom, her feet were frozen but felt like they were burning. She put her shoes back on to try to get some feeling back into her toes but was so focused on trying to warm them that she didn't hear the snow crunching under her feet until too late.

"Who goes there?" a guard shouted from the wall.

Kora froze. The warning bells rang. She didn't know what to do. A group of guards came running out from the garrison on the other side of the courtyard, torches flaming brightly. In the sudden light, Kora could not hide her shadow or keep her focus well enough to stay invisible. Her power wavered, and she saw the guards gaping at her.

"Lady Kora?" Nicodemo, the head guard, asked in disbelief. "What in the stars are you doing out here at this time of night?"

Kora hesitated. They didn't know. They couldn't possibly guess. "I ... couldn't sleep."

" You know the rules. No students allowed out after dark without an adult escort," Nicodemo reminded her. "Did you not think to light a lantern?"

"I was just practising my skills," she said lamely.

"What's this ruckus?" a familiar voice thundered behind her. Kora turned sheepishly to face her father. King Lukys, Uncle Kynon and half the teachers in the castle weren't far behind him.

"Kora! Of all the idiotic things! Just what did you think you were doing?"

Kora did not answer – she could feel the fear radiating off him. Giving no excuse was better than lying to her father. She'd never done it before.

"Go to bed this instant young lady. I'll deal with you in the morning!"

"Aaron, calm down." Uncle Lukys rubbed his temples and lay a hand on her father's arm. "Your family is safe here."

Kora saw the warring emotions on her father's face. Uncle Lukys was tempering his anger.

"Bed. Now."

Kora bowed her head in acquiescence and walked back towards the castle. She could hear the guards complaining to Uncle Lukys and his terse replies to them, but all she could think was that Pér was waiting for her and she would never arrive.

Chapter Thirteen

"Kitchen duty," her father told her the next morning. "I've spoken to Cook Tobias and it seems he is short-staffed. You will work in the kitchens for one week. He will expect you there before dawn every morning and you will work until it is time for your lessons to begin. You will return after the evening meal to help clean the dishes.

"Perhaps *that* will make you think twice before you alarm the guards with your thoughtless behaviour. You start now."

Kora lifted her chin defiantly, taking the sentence without a word. If her father found out what she had really been doing, the punishment was bound to be worse than a week in the kitchens.

Cook Tobias had run the kitchens as long as Kora could remember, and she had been running through his kitchen since she was old enough to roam the castle by herself. When she presented herself to him that morning, he pointed her over to Cook Palmyra.

The stern-faced cook looked her up and down. She was one of the younger cooks in the kitchen. Kora thought this week would be almost as much a punishment for the young cook as for herself.

"Have you ever done any cooking at all?" she asked doubtfully. Kora shook her head.

"Chopped vegetables?" She shook her head again.

Cook Palmyra covered her eyes with her hands and took a deep breath.

"Let's start you off peeling potatoes then," she finally decided. "Yasmina!"

The young kitchen maid who had scolded Kora all those months ago came running up, apron strings flapping behind her. She looked up at Kora with open-eyed curiosity. Kora gave her a half-hearted smile.

"Yasmina, Lady Kora will be joining us for the next week, morning and evening. She will shadow you. Give her all the potatoes you have to peel and show her how it's done."

Yasmina's eyes almost bulged out of her head. "Begging your pardon, Cook Palmyra, but what do I have to show her?"

Kora glanced at Cook Palmyra's scowl and decided to spare her from the conversation.

"I've never done anything in the kitchen before, Yasmina," Kora said quietly. "I don't even know what you use to peel potatoes."

"You don't know how to peel potatoes," Yasmina said slowly, as though she couldn't wrap her head around the thought. Then she looked Kora up and down. "Um ... well, you'll need an apron first. Your clothes are far too fine to get covered in starch."

Kora smiled and nodded, though she had no idea what Yasmina was talking about. She was soon to learn. Her first session lasted only an hour, but it felt much longer.

Yasmina handed her a knife and pointed to a bucket full of potatoes. Kora took the knife and looked from the knife to the potatoes with an overwhelming sense of dread.

"Those are for lunch. The peels go in that bucket and the potatoes go in that one, but mind you fill it with water first."

"Why?" Kora asked lamely.

Yasmina looked at her as though she was stupid. "To stop them going brown and wash off the starch, of course."

"Of course," Kora repeated quietly. "The starch. And how do I peel them?"

Yasmina laughed loudly. Kora knew the girl didn't mean to be cruel, but she couldn't help the flush burning her cheeks. Yasmina finally stopped laughing and stared incredulously at her.

"Oh, you *really* don't know how to peel them?"

Kora didn't answer.

"Well, you hold the potato like this. You could peel it any number of ways, but I find it easiest to start from the top and go around in a spiral. You miss less of the peel that way and don't need to go back over it."

Kora watched as Yasmina demonstrated with the first potato. It didn't look difficult at all. Yasmina almost made it look graceful. Feeling more confident than she had any right to be, Kora picked up a potato and set her knife to it. With her first slice, she cut deeply into her finger. She yelped in shock and pain as blood spilled out over the potato. Yasmina stared at her dumbly.

"Can you heal me?" Kora asked, gripping her finger tightly to slow the bleeding. Yasmina shook her head.

"Then can you find someone who can?" Kora gritted her teeth as the kitchen maid disappeared in a flurry of apron strings.

It wasn't long before Kora heard heavy footsteps approaching. She looked up from her bloody finger to see Cook Palmyra glaring down at her. Lamely, she held out her finger. Kora was expecting to have her finger completely healed, like they did in class, but Cook Palmyra only closed the wound to stop the bleeding. With some annoyance, Kora realised she meant to leave her like that.

"Could you perhaps heal it a little more?" she asked rather impolitely.

"No," came the stern reply. "If you've managed to cut yourself on your first try, I imagine there will be more to follow. I don't have the time or the energy to spend completely healing all of your wounds today."

Kora stared at her, dumbfounded.

"Um, best to fill up your bucket with water," Yasmina told Kora. Kora picked up the bucket and stormed off from her station, belatedly realising she didn't know where to get water from. She turned back to Yasmina who, thankfully, was watching her. The kitchen maid pointed her towards the sinks. There was a row of them against one wall. Kora looked at them curiously. Above each sink was a tap, but not like the ones in her bathtub. These taps had little handles on them. She placed her bucket under one of the taps and looked around. Further down, there was a boy filling up his own bucket. She watched as he twisted the handle to stop the water.

A little hesitantly, Kora twisted the handle above her bucket. Water came out in a thin trickle. She turned it further and further until the water was coming out so fast that it splashed all over her. Frantically, she turned the handle all the way in the opposite direction. The water stopped flowing, but too late. Kora's entire front was wet, and the bucket was near to overflowing. Angrily, she tipped some of the water out so that it wouldn't slosh all over her legs and drench her shoes as well.

When she tried to lift the bucket, she found it was too heavy. Kora threw her head back in frustration and balled up her fingers into a tight fist. Without a thought for whether it was appropriate, or even acceptable, Kora dumped a small portion of her power into the sink, under and around the bucket. She lifted it with practically no effort and walked over to where Yasmina waited for her, mouth gaping open.

"Don't show off, Kora," Cook Palmyra admonished her. "The kitchen staff don't have much power, so you best keep displays like that out of here."

Kora felt like screaming. She hadn't even been in the kitchen for an hour and had already been laughed at, cut her finger, wet her clothes and been reprimanded. The water in her bucket started bubbling before she could set it down and withdraw her power.

Yasmina pointed mutely at the bucket. Cook Palmyra followed her finger and sighed.

"And since you're so keen to show off your power, you can just siphon off that heat into the cauldrons over in those fireplaces. At least we won't need to wait an hour for them to boil today."

Kora seethed with anger and did as she was told. She was certain the heat of her anger was adding to the heat from the bucket in front of her. In the time it took her to breathe calmly again, four massive cauldrons were steaming away.

"Hm, a useful trait," Cook Palmyra grudgingly admitted. "You can do that every morning before you start on the potatoes. I suggest you get back to the peeling and, this time, try to be more careful with that paring knife."

Chapter Fourteen

The bell for morning lessons finally tolled. Kora tore off her apron and wiped her hands on it before tossing it into a pile of other dirty aprons. Doubtless the other aprons did not have so much blood on them.

She ran up the stairs to the classrooms and ran into Pér outside Mistress Chandrelle's room.

"What happened?" he asked.

"No now," Kora replied tersely. "I'll explain later."

Thankfully, Pér did not try to argue with her, but held the door open instead. Inside all the students were grouped in pairs. Kora saw Lishe and Nyssa sitting together. Her sister did not even glance in her direction. She would have to do something about that. Spending most evenings at Pér's house left little time for the two of them to talk. Nyssa might even have knocked on her door of an evening, thinking that Kora was ignoring her when Kora wasn't even there.

Kora decided to make more of an effort to spend time with Nyssa but, for now, she sat next to Pér.

"Let's continue to practise healing cuts and burns today," Mistress Chandrelle instructed them.

Kora looked down at her ruined hands. Pér would have his work cut out for him. She couldn't even remember how many times she'd cut herself while peeling potatoes that morning.

"What happened to you?" Pér asked when he saw her hands.

Mistress Chandrelle joined them at his exclamation. Kora clenched her fists and tried to hide them in the folds of her skirts.

"Show me."

Kora shrank away from the teacher's tone of voice, but there was no point in refusing so she laid her hands flat on her knees. The teachers had ways of forcing students to do their bidding.

"Right," Mistress Chandrelle said quietly. She turned to the class and announced in a louder voice, "Leave off working in pairs for now. Everyone gather around Kora. Today we will practise group healing."

Kora shook her head, a cold pool of dread welling up in her stomach. Her father had *promised* to talk to her teachers about her beliefs. It would have ensured that she was never put in a situation like this, where every student in her class would touch her skin and potentially have access to all her thoughts and moods.

"Mistress Chandrelle, I don't think that's necessary." She tried to say it in a confident, carefree voice, but it was so difficult with her heart pounding in her ears.

Mistress Chandrelle looked at her sharply. "Until you've mastered your skills and passed the rigorous tests to become a healing mistress, don't you dare presume to tell me what's necessary in my own classroom."

Kora cringed from her acidic rebuke. Her classmates teetered on the edge of their seats until Mistress Chandrelle motioned them over again. Kora looked at Pér helplessly. He, at least, knew what was going on inside her at that very moment, but she knew he was as helpless to do anything about it as she was.

"Kora has clearly sustained a number of cuts this morning," Mistress Chandrelle informed the class. "By the looks of it, the cuts were roughly closed over to stop the bleeding. Until we delve into her hands to investigate, we will not know if anything further was done.

"As the surface area is too small for everyone to touch, some of you will need to place your hands on her arms, or other exposed skin, and find your way to the cuts. I will be in there with you but will refrain from any action unless I think you are making matters worse.

"You will need to follow one voice for this group healing to work effectively. Do I have any volunteers?"

Kora's stomach lurched as she saw Lishe's hand shoot up. Pér and Morwenna also raised their hands. After a swift nudge from Lishe, Nyssa also raised her hand, clearly reluctant. Kora wished Pér would be chosen, but he was not the most skilled in their class.

"Nyssa, I'm glad to see you volunteer for such a difficult task. You may lead this healing session."

Kora saw the flicker of terror cross her sister's face. They had never performed a group healing led by a student before. It was a dangerous process and needed a skilled leader. Nyssa was certainly powerful, but Kora doubted she was skilled enough.

Kora bit her lip and unfurled her hands. She caught Nyssa's eye. Her sister gave her a reassuring smile, but it did little to ease Kora's nerves. Nyssa placed her right hand over most of Kora's left hand. Immediately after that, other students began pulling up her sleeve to place their hands on her skin, their power surging down towards Nyssa's power and Kora's cuts.

Panicked, Kora withdrew her power behind her wall and strengthened it further. She did not want anyone in her class getting a glimpse of her thoughts or feelings. It surprised Kora to feel her elbows both gripped tightly by someone. She looked down to see Pér's hands. All the other students had their hands closer towards her wounds.

With a sudden rush of relief, Kora realised what Pér was doing. She could no longer feel the other students' power coursing through her – he had effectively created a barrier. She fought not to whimper in thanks and watched, almost detached, as her cuts were healed by her classmates.

Mistress Chandrelle held Kora and Pér back after class.

"I know that was a difficult lesson for you, Kora, but you should not have allowed Pér to waste this opportunity just to spare your feelings. We do not often have injuries that can be worked on by such large groups. By creating a barrier – yes, *of course* I noticed what you did – Pér did not get to join in the healing himself. I am very disappointed in the both of you. It was a foolish decision."

"It was *not* a foolish decision," Kora snapped. "If you *knew* how difficult this lesson was for me, that means my father has spoken to you and you chose to ignore him."

Mistress Chandrelle's eyes narrowed. "Pér, you may leave us now."

Kora did not look away from the healing mistress, but she could sense Pér's reticence to leave her.

"Now, Pér!" Mistress Chandrelle raised her voice.

The door clicked closed behind him as Pér left the room.

"As for you, young lady, I *earned* my position through hard work and dedication. I was not made a healing mistress by the grace of your father and I will not be dictated to by your family.

"I will run my lessons as I see fit. If you have a problem with that, your father is within his rights to request private tuition from another healing teacher for you. Until that day, you will not strip away every opportunity Pér has in this class to spare your precious sensibilities. Is that clear?"

"Crystal," Kora replied through gritted teeth. She turned on her heel and left the room, not waiting to be dismissed.

Pér was waiting for her at the end of the hall, far enough to duck out of Mistress Chandrelle's sight if she'd happened to be the first to exit the room. Kora went with him down to the dining hall in stormy silence.

The warm and comforting smell of cooked vegetables wafted over to her as she walked through the massive wooden doors. Determined to sample the food she had helped to prepare this morning, Kora filled more than half her plate with potatoes, then filled the rest with other vegetables.

Kora spotted her cousins and sister sitting at their usual tables. She did not want to speak with any of them right now. Instead, she led Pér to an empty table, far away from them.

"You still haven't explained how you got those injuries," Pér nudged her softly, while they were eating. "Or why I didn't see you last night."

Kora placed her fork down gently and explained what had happened. "And so, this morning, father told me to report to the kitchen. My punishment is to work there every morning and evening for a week. Though I think I'm proving to be more trouble than I'm worth."

"Kitchen duty?" Pér chuckled. "I guess that puts an end to our evenings together then."

Kora frowned.

"You'll be fine," he told her gently.

"I know," Kora replied tersely, then sighed heavily. "I know I will. I haven't had nightmares in weeks now. But it was ..."

"Nice?"

Kora looked at Pér fondly. "Yes. It was nice, but I don't *need* it anymore."

Pér leaned in towards her. Kora instinctively leaned in to kiss him but pulled away before their lips touched. She didn't want a repeat of last time. Even though she knew what he dreamed for the future, she didn't want to see it. Not again.

Once he realised she wasn't going to kiss him, Pér leaned back in his seat, nonchalantly.

"So, what did Mistress Chandrelle say after I left?"

Kora gritted her teeth. "It basically boils down to my father and I deciding whether to have private lessons or let her keep using me as she pleases in class."

Pér whistled through his teeth. "Tough choice. Do you think your father would let you have private lessons?"

"I don't know." Kora shrugged. "He cared enough to talk to my teachers in the first place, but we never discussed what would happen if they refused to listen to him. We don't have another healing class for a few days. Maybe I'll have learnt to use a knife properly by then and it won't be an issue."

"If not?" Pér pressed her.

Kora huffed. "If *not*, then I suppose I'll ask father to let me have private lessons."

"Careful, Kora. Once you do that with one class, you'll be more inclined to do it with your other classes."

"So?" Kora replied defensively.

"Well, do you really think it's a good idea? You're already isolated from a lot of lintep just by being a Lady. Discontinuing group lessons will only isolate you further."

"Like you said, I'm already isolated. What difference would it make now?" Kora got up and left the dining hall, not bothering to finish eating the potatoes she had laboured over so hard to bring to the table.

Chapter Fifteen

"Father, *please*." Kora had made her case, but her father had not agreed. "You know how it makes me feel. I don't like people being able to jump into my mind more easily because they are allowed, *by my teachers*, to have skin contact with me. I don't want any of them to be able to influence my moods. Why can't you understand that?"

Her father remained seated, looking up as Kora paced back and forth in front of him. "I do understand, my dear, but I disagree. No, hear me out now. You may think you will always have the choice in life to stop lintep from having skin contact with you, that it won't be a problem if I allow you to have private lessons, but that is not the case.

"Presuming you live out your days in Illaria, think of the fact that you will need to choose how best to serve our people. If you become a healer yourself, you will have constant skin contact with others. If you become a mistress of any of our skills, it may become necessary for you to have contact with other teachers or, indeed, with recalcitrant students.

"Now imagine I allow you to have private lessons so you never learn how to properly defend yourself against those situations. I will have failed in my duty as your father to allow you to so easily evade a vital part of your training.

"My answer is no, Kora, and it will remain so as long as your training continues."

Kora's blood boiled. She hated the way her anger turned so easily into heat. She leaked out a tendril of her power towards the fireplace and allowed all the excess heat to fuel the fire. The flames flew high, the wood cracked in the sudden temperature change. Kora turned away from the sudden unbearable heat to see the disappointed look on her father's face.

Control your temper.

It was one of the lessons he had tried to drum into her – into all of them. She used to be good at it, though never as good as Fredryck. But since their return to Illaria, she had found it almost impossible.

Without another word, Kora strode out of her father's chambers. As she rounded the corner to her own chambers, she saw Nyssa walking down the hallway, quickly and with her head down as though she didn't want to be noticed.

"Nyssa, wait!" called out Kora. Nyssa stumbled, but did not stop or even look back. Kora ran after her. "Where are you going?"

"To study," Nyssa replied shortly.

"At this hour?" Kora asked bemused. She had already spent hours in the kitchen cleaning all the dishes from the last meal of the day and then argued with her father for longer than she cared to think about. It must be near midnight.

"We won't be disturbed at this hour," Nyssa said, walking quickly down the stairs. Kora followed her, not trusting her sister.

"Who is 'we'?"

Nyssa did not answer.

"Please don't tell me you're actually practising with Lishe," Kora hissed, her voice echoing off the twisted stairwells. "Nyssa, there are better people to practise with. *I'll* practise with you."

"You," laughed Nyssa as they exited onto the next landing. "You couldn't even trust me enough in leading the healing on your hand this morning to let Pér take part. You thought I would let our entire class run amok in your mind rather than focus on our task. Why would I ever want to practise with you?"

"That's not fair!" Kora grabbed at Nyssa's sleeve, forcing her sister to stop and face her. "I was unprepared for that ... and scared."

"You don't think *I* was scared?" Nyssa asked incredulously. "I've never been involved with a group healing, let alone led one. But I did that *for you*."

Kora let go of the sleeve bunched up in her fist. "I'm sorry, Nyssa. I didn't think of that."

Nyssa's face softened. "We're sisters, Kora. We're all we both have left of our siblings. Why can't you just let me be there for you? Even just sometimes."

Kora nodded, hot tears stinging her eyes. Through blurred vision, she saw Nyssa smile and turn back down the way she had been headed.

"Nyssa," she called out. Her sister stopped but did not turn. "Let *me* be there for you too. I don't trust Lishe. If you're going to train with her, let me come too."

Together, Kora and Nyssa walked into Lishe's room. It was not the first time Kora had been in a student lodging, but Lishe's room was not at all like Luisella's. Luisella's room had sketched portraits of her family adorning the walls, but Lishe's walls were bare. Where Luisella's room had an odd assembly of trinkets from her house on her desk and colourful clothes tumbling out of her clothes chest, Lishe's desk was clear of everything except books, parchment, an inkwell and a quill. It seemed there was nothing here to remind Lishe of her home, or of anything other than her studies.

"Kora's joining us tonight." Nyssa attempted to make the comment sound matter of fact, but Kora could hear her voice wobble and knew Lishe had heard it too.

Lishe raised an eyebrow and stared at Kora for a long time. Kora twitched under her stare and fought the urge to rub her arms. Lishe made her skin crawl, but Nyssa was worth the discomfort.

"What are we practising tonight?" Kora asked lightly.

"How to defend against a breach in your walls," Lishe answered smoothly. "Since you're new, *you* can go first."

Kora fought the urge to look at Nyssa. She swallowed the bile in her mouth and nodded. She withdrew behind her wall, and lined the inner side with her power, pushing outwards, feeling for any hint of penetration.

Wisps of power curled into every crevice like smoke. Every now and then, she felt a sharp and clumsy jab. The two sets of powers were unmistakable. Lishe's smoky power was sneakier – if there was even a crack in Kora's wall, she would find it. Nyssa seemed not to be looking for a way to sneak in but was instead content to try to batter her wall down.

If it had only been one or the other, Kora felt certain she could have withstood their attempt. But she could not hold out against both of them while sheltered behind her wall. Gathering her strength and her power, Kora let a portion flood out, overwhelming the attackers before creating a large shield out of her power.

Nyssa's power smashed against the shield, while Lishe's smoky wisps curled around the side and came onwards towards Kora. Breathing rapidly, Kora stretched the shield further, forcing Lishe to withdraw her power. Not trusting that the vile lintep would stop there, Kora stretched her shield out to completely surround herself, effectively creating a dome of power around her. Lishe's wisps tried to get under her power from the bottom, but sandstone was not laid in slats like wood – she could not even scratch her way under Kora's power.

Kora smiled, calmer now. Her breath finally slowed to normal. But then Nyssa hurled her power against the bubble like a battering ram. The wind was knocked out of her lungs as she fell backwards. Lishe immediately took advantage of the situation and sent her smoky tendrils to Kora's mind, stealing into it before she had a chance to defend herself. Kora couldn't breathe. Her lungs were burning, her ribs were bruised.

Nyssa was by her side calling out to her, but Kora couldn't focus on her for the insidious tendrils of power now running through her mind, trying to latch on to any nugget of information.

Out! she roared with her power, shoving out in all directions.

Kora coughed and gasped in air. She found herself sprawled on the floor, Nyssa by her side. Lishe was pinned against the wall by some invisible force. It took Kora a moment to realise that it was *her* power holding Lishe up and away from her. Lishe did not look at all uncomfortable – she was smiling.

"So, daddy won't let you have private lessons?" Lishe laughed cruelly. "Poor little lady."

Kora's lips curled as she shoved Nyssa's fidgeting hands away from her. She pulled out a long tendril of her power and drove it straight into Lishe's mind.

"Mother, why don't you stop him?" Lishe asked. Her mother was huddled in a corner, bruised and bloodied.

"I can't," she sobbed in reply. "You know I don't have enough power."

"Then leave him!"

"I can't," her mother repeated over and over again.

Kora took a moment to look around the memory. The house was tiny – a single room with bedrolls bunched up in a corner behind a small wooden table and chairs. The kitchen was nothing more than a sink and a stove.

"I'll do something then," Lishe said quietly. "I'll tell someone, and they'll make him stop hurting you."

"You can't." Her mother stretched a hand out towards her. "What will people think?"

"Our neighbours must already think things." Lishe shied away from the hand. "Even if you've stopped screaming, they must hear what he does to you through these ridiculous excuses for walls."

Kora drew back from the memory and released Lishe from her power. The bile seeped into her mouth with its bitter edge. She ran to the arrow-slit window and spat it out. Her hand caught at the edge of the desk. She used it to steady herself as she turned back to face Lishe.

"I'm sorry," she said weakly.

"What for?" Lishe replied coldly. "He never laid a hand on *me*."

"Who never laid a hand on you?" Nyssa asked in confusion. "What are you two talking about?"

Kora ignored Nyssa's question. "I think that's enough for tonight. Let's go, Nyssa."

"But I haven't had a turn yet ..."

"Not. Tonight." Kora pulled her by the sleeve, not leaving it to chance that Nyssa would follow her.

The two of them walked quietly up the stairs. Kora one step in front, constantly looking back to see if Lishe was following them. Instead of leaving Nyssa in her own room, Kora held her door open until Nyssa walked in. Carefully, she locked the door behind them.

"What's going on, Kora?" Nyssa asked, voice trembling. Kora sat her down on the chaise and set about making a pot of chamomile tea.

"Kora!" she cried out impatiently.

Kora looked up at her blankly and went back to making tea. She could still feel the terror from Lishe's memory – her guilty relief that her father only ever attacked her mother.

She rubbed her hands over her face then brought one cup to Nyssa, and another for herself.

"I don't think we should try that skill with Lishe anymore," Kora decided. "It isn't fair to do it when she has so little power compared to us."

"What happened, Kora?" Nyssa asked, warily.

Kora sat down beside her sister and explained everything, except for the exact details of the memory she'd seen. Nyssa refilled both their cups twice, but the chamomile was having no effect on Kora's nerves at all.

"You're quite shaken, Kora," Nyssa finally broke the silence. "Surely the memory didn't scare you that much."

Kora shook her head. "It isn't just the memory. It's Lishe. She hardly has any power, but she's so ... sneaky with it. Did you even notice how she was attacking me?"

Nyssa shook her head. Kora wasn't surprised. The way Nyssa had tried to ram down her walls, she wouldn't have noticed anything as subtle as wisps of smoke floating by her.

"I'm just glad she doesn't have much power. I'd be terrified of her if she did."

She noticed Nyssa didn't disagree. What had the two of them gotten up to before Kora joined in their practice sessions?

Chapter Sixteen

Kora peeled the potatoes ever so slowly the next morning. She did not want to give any of her teachers the idea that group healings or group *anything* should be carried out on her because of her injured hands.

Peeling slowly or quickly, Kora still cut herself. The only difference it made was that Cook Palmyra became so frustrated with her slow progress that she set her to fetching herbs instead. Kora was almost as bad at that as peeling potatoes. The only herb she could readily identify was chamomile and *that* was not used in everyday cooking.

Mint infused peas became basil infused peas. Potatoes with rosemary became potatoes with thyme. Rice with coriander became rice with parsley.

The worst thing she did was eventually drawn to the attention of the entire kitchen and the dining hall. She'd been asked to add a bowl of chopped sweet red peppers to the vegetable stew. She'd walked over to the stew and saw two bowls of chopped red slivers. Assuming there had been a mistake as to how many bowls there were, she'd tipped both bowls in.

When Cook Palmyra asked Yasmina to taste the stew for seasoning later that morning, the poor girl started coughing and spluttering.

"You daft ninny!" Cook Palmyra shouted. "You put a whole bowl of chilli in the stew! It's completely ruined."

Kora fetched milk and a hunk of bread for Yasmina, and apologised over and over for her mistake. The poor girl could barely breathe. Tears streamed down her red, sweaty face.

When time came to serve the meal, Cook Palmyra had forced Kora to accompany her. "Now, you can tell them why there is no vegetable stew today."

Kora had stared at the dining hall filling with students, teachers and her family. The blood drained from her face, her palms had been clammy.

"Due to a kitchen mishap, there will be no vegetable stew today," Kora said loudly.

"What kind of kitchen mishap?" Gethin had called out. Kora could have just slapped him.

"There was a touch too much chilli added to it."

"By who?" he jeered.

"By me, you halfwit," Kora shouted.

"At least I'm not the halfwit that ruined the meal for everyone."

Kora had bitten her lip to stop herself from crying in front of all those people. She'd turned on her heel and headed straight back to the kitchen, not allowing Gethin to make any further jokes at her expense.

Later that evening, after she had lived down the shame of her kitchen calamity, Kora stared at the stack of books on her desk. They were the ones she had borrowed from the library months ago. Some of them had piqued her interest, but many of them contained the same old drivel everyone in Illaria believed about humans. She was sick of reading those books – sick of everyone assuming they had a right to use their powers on defenceless humans. It was bad enough they thought it was reasonable to use their powers on other lintep without asking, but at least most lintep had the training to shield their minds if they so desired.

Angrily, she piled them high and slid them off the desk, carefully placing her hands underneath so they didn't fall to the ground. It was time to take them back to the library.

"It's about time you returned these, young lady," the librarian said in mock anger. He turned to his ledger to mark them each off as returned, but then waggled a finger at her. "Don't think I've forgotten about that unmarked book just because it has no title. I will expect that back in due course as well."

Kora walked back to her room in mingled curiosity and worry. She had forgotten all about the unmarked book and could not remember seeing it in her rooms. Back at her desk, Kora searched for the book. It did not take her long to find it on the floor, opened with pages bent back. It must have fallen off her desk while she sorted through the rest of the books.

She picked it up, closed it carefully, certain that Guiscard would reprimand her for crushing the pages, and placed it on the little table beside her chaise.

Before turning her attention completely to the book, Kora made herself a lavender tea, using the heat of her anger to warm it. Untouched, the tea went cold as she read.

I find myself at a loss now that Rilla is dead. Our parents are adamant that all humans are as thoughtless and vicious as some of the ones we have come across, but I do not agree. I don't think Edamo does either. Rilla helped us see that there was more to these humans than meets the eye. Most of them are such sweet, caring creatures.

I feel a jolt of anger every time I see a lintep use their power on these poor defenceless people. It's no wonder some of them attack us with no thought. It must feel like we are doing the same to them when we use our power on them.

I have resolved never to use my power on another human without their express permission beforehand. I do not know if that will make them trust me more, but I can only hope it will.

~

I have resolved to continue Rilla's work, in a way. She wanted to integrate humans with lintep, but it appears that will not work – at least not right now. Instead, I want to create a safe place for humans. A place where they can live without magic, without the fear that a lintep will use their powers on them. I haven't worked out the details yet, but I'm working on it.

Kora stared at the neat and confident script lining the pages. Could this possibly be the writing of Ophélie? How had her great-aunt's journal ended up in the library? A hundred questions ran through Kora's mind. She ignored them all and re-read that first page.

With a trembling hand, Kora closed the book. She didn't know whether she felt pleased that others felt the same way she did about how lintep used their powers, or angry that even Ophélie and Rilla had not been able to change their parents' minds. It did not give her much hope for her own future in Illaria. Things would *never* change. How could they when so very many people did not agree?

It was a lazy afternoon. Most of the castle occupants had gone home for the two-day break. Others were outside, enjoying the rare sunlit winter day.

The five of them sat huddled in the library. Kora had sent out a message to her cousins and friends early that morning. They hadn't spent nearly so much time together lately as she would have liked, especially with her father keeping an extra close eye on her after the fiasco that landed her with kitchen duty for a week.

"How do you know any of this, Kora?" Braedan asked, a little abrasively. "Ophélie is not *your* grandmother. I would have been told more about her than you."

Kora did not want to reveal her source. Not yet. Perhaps not ever. There was still so much of the book that she had not read. Until she knew exactly what it contained, she would not show them. If she did, it was likely Uncle Kynon would confiscate it before she had a chance to finish reading it. Kora was *not* willing to let that happen. Not when she had found someone who felt so completely understood how she felt and strongly agreed with her.

"Never mind how I know," Kora waved the issue aside. "The point is, I'm not the only one who has ever felt this way."

"I understand, Kora dear, but how does that change things?" Aislen asked gently. "You can't simply tell our people that Princess Ophélie felt this way too and expect them all to change their minds. Especially not after ..."

Kora looked at her sharply. "Especially not after some of my family was murdered by humans. Is that what you were going to say?"

"Well, yes. It is."

"Do you know why they were killed?" Kora asked. Their shocked expressions spoke volumes. Thinking back on it, she had only told Uncle Lukys which town they had come from, which inn they had patronised and the appearance of any humans she could remember. She hadn't told anyone what she suspected about the reason.

"Well, I don't know if it's definitely the reason, but it's the only thing I can think of," Kora started. "We stayed at an inn in Hedgefall. I didn't think anything of it at the time, but we were talking about Rilla and what she had tried to do for humans. The conversation *may* have got a little heated when Father and I started debating certain things to do with her and how it changed a lot of people's view of humans.

"I know a few humans took notice of the conversation because Mother hushed us, just not quickly enough. Their heads were turned towards us when I looked around. Father and I stopped arguing, but the damage had been done. They must have realised by then that we were related to Rilla. It's the only reason I can think for why they would have bothered tracking us until Adina and Fredryck were alone."

"And you *still* think you shouldn't use your power on them?" Luisella asked in surprise. Kora nodded.

"Absolutely!" she almost shouted. "I *hate* it when anyone uses their power on me when I haven't asked them to or given them permission. The only thing that makes it almost bearable for me is that I'm powerful and skilled enough to make most people leave me alone if I want them to. Humans don't have that ability.

"Imagine if your mind teacher told someone in your class, let's say your least favourite person, to dive into your mind and find out everything they could about you. What would you do?"

"That would never happen," Braedan pointed out.

"But just imagine it did," Kora insisted. "What would you do?"

She saw Luisella hesitate. Even Braedan and Pér hesitated. Aislen held Kora's gaze steadily. They both had more power than their three friends. They would be able to contain everything they needed to in their minds.

"I ... I suppose I would protest," Luisella finally said.

Kora nodded. "And if they took no notice of you and told the student to go ahead. What would you do?"

"I don't like this game, Kora," Luisella whimpered.

"That's the whole point," Kora said, pointing at Luisella. "You don't like it, but at least you have some power to stop some of it from happening. Humans don't have any defence at all. Can you really blame them for thinking lintep are assaulting them when they don't ask permission to use their power? Can you blame them for wanting to attack us before we get the chance to do something to them?"

Pér cleared his throat. "I see what you mean, Kora. But I do not think we can call them blameless when they attack us."

"That's not what I'm saying," Kora grew frustrated. "I'm not saying they're blameless. But I can understand them. *I* felt under attack in our own healing classes and father won't let me take private lessons. *I'm* going to be uncomfortable in every one of my lessons from now on because I know Mistress Chandrelle will ignore my feelings. She already has."

There was a startled cough from Guiscard's desk. Kora should have known better than to think the librarian was keeping himself occupied with the books open in front of him.

"What do you propose to do about it?" Aislen asked before Kora could say anything to Guiscard.

"What can I do?" Kora asked helplessly. "I can't have private lessons and I can't quit my lessons without father's approval. All I can do is hope not to have another injury so bad that it requires a group healing. My kitchen duty is over, so at least *that* shouldn't cause any more problems."

"That's just your healing class," Aislen pointed out. "What about the others?"

Kora hesitated. "Father spoke to all of my teachers about my ... feelings on the matter. I think most of them have agreed not to press me."

Aislen didn't comment. Neither did the others. Kora knew she had no real choice in the matter – so did the others. If her teachers decided to go against her wishes, they were within their rights to do so.

I can't stay here, Kora thought to herself. *I can't live like this.*

Chapter Seventeen

The marketplace was a hive of activity as Kora and Pér meandered through it. Neither of them had said a word since leaving the library. Kora tried to imagine what Pér must think of her, defending humans when they had so savagely attacked her family.

"Is that why you won't kiss me?"

Kora blinked, shook her head and stared at Pér.

"What?" she asked in confusion.

"Is that why you won't kiss me?" he repeated himself. "Because you think I'll use my power on you."

"No." Kora shook her head. How could she possibly explain it to him without making things worse? She smiled half-heartedly at some of the townsfolk who waved to her as she passed by. "Can we talk about this somewhere quieter?"

Pér led her to his house. Kora raised an eyebrow at him.

"My parents are at our stall in the marketplace. This is as quiet as you will ever find my house."

Kora walked in through the front door. It amazed her that his entire house could fit in her private chambers. Yet, it felt so comfortable, so homely.

She watched as Pér filled a teapot and set it to boil over the fireplace. They both had more than enough power to warm the water themselves, but she appreciated that it gave him time to prepare the rose buds in their teacups.

The teapot whistled over the fire and Pér took it away from the fire with a large metal hook. He placed it gently on the wooden counter and used a bundle of rags to protect his hand as he poured the boiling water over the flowers. Kora followed him to the cushioned chaise across from the fireplace and sat beside him.

"So?" Pér looked at her expectantly.

So, she thought, *where to begin.*

"I was unprepared when we kissed. I had been trying something with my power and didn't realise it was still all around me, otherwise I never would have ..." she trailed off.

"You never would have shown me as much as you accidentally did," Pér finished the sentence for her. "And you think that's the reason I showed you everything I did, as a return favour?"

"Well, yes. Isn't it?" Kora's heart beat faster.

"No, but I can see how you thought that." Pér reached out and took her hand. Kora's skin tingled where he touched her, but there was no power there. She looked up at him in surprise. "I realise it makes you uncomfortable, but you never gave me the chance to show you that I can keep my power to myself."

Kora's cheeks were burning. Her heart was beating so loudly she was certain Pér must be able to hear it. Slowly, she curled her fingers around his hand. While she was looking at their hands, he took her by surprise and kissed her forehead. His breath was hot against her skin. She tore her eyes away from their hands and over to his lips. They were so close to her. Kora felt his thumb tracing her lips, tickling them.

With a smile, she tilted her head up, away from his hand and kissed him with an urgency that surprised her. It was so different from that first time when their powers had mingled. This time, she felt safer – not at all guilty.

Late that night, Kora finished reading the journal. Safe havens. That's what Ophélie had wanted to create. Little "paradises" where humans could live, free from magic. Free from the types of people that Kora now struggled with on an almost daily basis. It was difficult to believe, but Ophélie had found a way to save humans from the fear of magic.

The final pages of the book contained a map. Hand drawn and detailed with marks to show where the little paradises had been created. Kora studied it carefully. There was one near Illaria, not quite half-way to Hedgefall. It was likely her family had passed it going to and from Silvaren without noticing it was there.

Kora went to close the book when she was done looking at the map, but something caught her eye in the margin. It looked like a short poem. She opened the book to the very last page and continued reading.

When a crystal heart beats in the body of another,
Their song will destroy that which was created.
Every being will bow down to the child of Paradise,
All will hail Rilla.

Kora read the short passage over and over. It made no sense. Guiscard might know, but she couldn't go to him at this hour of the night. The library would certainly be closed by now.

She tossed and turned all night, impatiently waiting for dawn to break – and a reasonable time to find the librarian. Kora knew that Guiscard lived in the castle, but she had never visited him in his own chambers before. She realised with a pang of annoyance that she did not know which chambers were his.

As with all castle lodgers, Guiscard's chambers would be on the second level, just below the royal chambers. Kora walked down the stairs, book in hand, then down the long hallways, looking for any hint that a particular chamber might be the librarian's.

She should have known better. There were none. The only room on the lodgers' level that had any sort of marking was the elf ambassador's room. There was a carving of a tree on the door. Kora had never understood why until she visited Silvaren. The thought of the elegant, glossy black trees with various coloured leaves and flowers brought a smile to her face.

Before her visit, trees had just been trees. She had never thought they could have a life of their own and, admittedly, normal trees didn't, but the trees in Silvaren weren't normal. Magic seemed to flow through the entire forest like a stream, meandering in and around the trees and elves. It gave the forest a unique atmosphere. Kora remembered feeling safe there. Perhaps she could return one day and feel safe again.

"Watch where you're walking!"

Kora looked up just in time to see Gethin. Her hand accidentally brushed his as he shouldered his way past. Kora snatched her hand away, but it was too late. She knew her mind was shielded well enough to have guarded against the accidental touch – it always was – but Gethin was not so cautious.

Once, just once, I wish she would notice me! What does she see in Pér? If she would just see me, she would have no time for that musical oaf!

45

Kora turned to see him hurry away without another word. Had she just imagined that? Had Master Flyndar known about this when he lectured them in class all those months ago? Is this why Morwenna had reprimanded Kora for her harsh words about Gethin?

Bemused, Kora turned and walked straight into Guiscard. The librarian overbalanced and reached out to grab Kora's hand. She reached out at the same time and caught his hand, pulling him back upright before he fell. No unguarded thoughts flew into her mind this time. Hurriedly, still not trusting their skin contact, Kora released his hand.

"I was just looking for you," she said quickly. "I wanted to ask you about that unmarked book."

Guiscard eyed her closely. "That unmarked book I asked you to return months ago?"

Kora nodded sheepishly. Guiscard sighed.

"What is it then?"

"I think I'd better show you in the library," Kora said cautiously.

Kora watched as Uncle Lukys leafed through the pages. Guiscard had called him down as soon as he'd realised what it was Kora had found.

"It's certainly Aunt Ophélie's," Uncle Lukys confirmed. "I don't know what it was doing in the library though. Surely, there were better places for it."

"I don't care about that." Kora waved his concern aside. "What I want to know is if either of you know what this means."

She turned to the back page and read out the short passage. It still puzzled her, no matter how many times she read it over. Uncle Lukys and Guiscard shared a worried look as she read it out to them.

"What is it?" she asked.

"Nothing to concern you," Uncle Lukys said quickly.

"If you don't tell me what it is, I'll go and ask father or Uncle Kynon instead," Kora threatened.

"It's a prophecy," Guiscard said, despite Uncle Lukys glaring at him.

"A prophecy? About what?"

"We think it's to do with these paradises Ophélie created. The prophecy came about soon after they were created."

"But that doesn't make any sense." Kora looked at the prophecy again and shook her head. "This makes it sound like the paradises Ophélie created will be destroyed."

"It does appear to be the case," Uncle Lukys agreed.

"But why?" Kora asked in confusion. Guiscard and Uncle Lukys shared another look.

"We don't know," Guiscard admitted. "Ophélie created them many, many years ago. What you've found here – in this book – this is the most information we have."

Kora looked at the book in her hands. It wasn't very thick, but Ophélie had crammed in as much as she could. What could have gone so terribly wrong with the paradises that a prophecy to end them had already been voiced before Ophélie was killed?

"Kora, you're not getting any silly ideas, are you?" Uncle Lukys asked her warily.

"Of course not, Uncle Lukys," she replied sweetly.

Uncle Lukys and Guiscard shared a look and then glared at her.

"Oh honestly, I haven't even finished my training yet. Why would I do anything silly before I take advanced classes in everything?"

It was not a good answer, but it was all she could give them. At least they seemed disinclined to argue the matter with her when she was not in a position to act on any decision she might make.

Chapter Eighteen

The months passed slowly. Kora's routine became predictable, if not mundane. She tried to stay out of trouble. She attended her lessons, giving her teachers as little reason as possible to purposely make the other students use their powers on her in a way she was uncomfortable with. It still happened, but at least it wasn't on a regular basis. Only Mistress Chandrelle seemed to try to find reasons for their class to do group sessions and place Kora in the thick of it.

She spent many evenings with Nyssa and Lishe. They often attempted things that she would rather have nothing to do with, but Kora refused to let Nyssa go alone for fear of what Lishe would convince her to do. Or, if she was honest with herself, what Lishe would do to Nyssa.

The rare afternoons she spent in the library with Aislen, Braedan, Luisella and Pér were her favourite times. Even if they did not agree with her whole-heartedly, they at least understood her point of view. She even heard them defending her beliefs to others.

But mostly, Kora thought about Ophélie. She had a horrible longing inside of her. She wished, more than anything, that she had known Ophélie. She just *knew* they would have gotten along. Ophélie would have understood Kora – they were so very similar.

The more Kora thought about Ophélie, the more she thought about the paradises. Could she find them? Could she figure out why there was a prophecy to destroy them? It seemed hardly anyone outside her family even knew the prophecy existed, and none of them would ever consider leaving Illaria to find out what had happened.

Kora began to plan. She spent every free moment she had in the library, finding out as much about the Outworld as possible. She withdrew from her friends, her sister, her father. The only people who still made an effort to spend time with her were her closest circle of friends – Aislen, Braedan, Luisella and Pér.

Pér. Things had been interesting between them of late. He knew she was hiding something, but he never expressly asked her about it. She was glad. She didn't know if she'd be able to lie to him and she certainly didn't want to tell him what she was planning. She wouldn't let him ruin his life for her.

Kora planned to finish her training before making her final decision. She wanted to at least know that she was as skilled as she would ever be and could protect herself if necessary. But the stars knew she understood well enough that things didn't always turn out the way you hoped they would.

It was an autumn afternoon, just over two years since the deaths of her mother and siblings. The wind had picked up and felt like it was blowing straight of the snow-capped Drakos and Lesa Mountains. Kora had felt on edge all day. She couldn't concentrate.

Master Amyas had invited Master Elwood, with his students, to do a combined lesson. It made sense, really – the mind and practical powers often went hand in hand. Kora knew the masters liked to keep the students on their toes by changing things around sometimes.

Normally, she wouldn't have cared, but there was one student who kept pushing the boundary. Arawn took things too far. Whenever Master Elwood took their lessons, the focus was on balance. With mind powers, the balance was listening and speaking, projecting and seeing. With practical powers, it was all push and pull. Today, they were attempting to project images into each other's minds.

Kora and Luisella were working together. Even though Lishe and Nyssa were in the same class, Kora did not try to work with either of them any more than she already did of an evening. She felt safer with Luisella – calmer.

Luisella smiled knowingly when Kora sent her an image of a door painted with jacarandas. They both knew whose door it was and how Kora's feelings towards the resident had grown.

Kora blushed deeply when Luisella then sent her an image of Pér. She had envisaged him perfectly. His lopsided smile, his messy hair, his tall, muscular form and the eyes that stared into her like they knew everything there was to know about her. Even in this mental image, Kora felt slightly intimidated by those eyes. Did Pér have any idea what she was planning?

"Kora, what's wrong?" Luisella whispered. "You've gone pale."

Kora tried to brush it off. "I forgot to eat this morning," she lied.

"I was in the dining hall," Luisella told her. "I *saw* you eat more than any one person should be able to consume in one meal. What's wrong?"

Kora was saved from replying by an outburst from Morwenna.

"Stop sending me those horrible images!" she yelled. "I don't want to see any of that."

Everyone stopped what they were doing and turned to see what was happening. Masters Amyas and Elwood walked swiftly over to Morwenna and Arawn.

"What's the meaning of this?" Master Amyas inquired with a steel-edged voice.

"Arawn keeps showing me things I'd rather not describe, even after I told him not to," Morwenna complained.

The masters shared a serious look, then Master Elwood nodded. The uneasiness in Kora grew stronger. Master Amyas turned to Arawn with his hands on his hips.

"Arawn, we do not generally act as tyrants, but if this behaviour continues, we will ensure that you cannot participate anymore."

"And how are you going to stop me?" Arawn asked snidely.

"Try it again and you'll find out." Master Amyas' tone was threatening. Kora had never seen him look so frightening before.

Arawn looked like he was weighing his options. Eventually, he shrugged and turned back to Morwenna.

"Daffodils and daisies then?" he asked in a horribly insulting tone.

Kora caught Morwenna's eye. She wished she had the courage to say she'd swap with her, but she could not purposely put herself in such an awful situation. Arawn would *never* respect the way she felt about how lintep used their powers.

"I'll work with Arawn." Lishe's voice rang out through the classroom.

Kora looked over to see the eagerness on her face as she stood up. A shiver went down her spine. There was something dreadfully wrong with Lishe. If it weren't for Nyssa, Kora would have nothing to do with her – *ever*.

"I do not think that would be advisable, Lishe," Master Elwood told her. "Arawn must learn to work with students who do not wish to give him the time of day. And, unfortunately, Morwenna must learn to work with students she would rather have nothing to do with."

Kora breathed a sigh of relief that she and Luisella had gone for the same table when they walked through the door. She couldn't imagine being paired with a student like Arawn – or more to the point, she could very well imagine it and did not like what she saw.

Arawn arrogantly tilted his chin up. "I don't think you can stop me. You're full of hot air."

Within seconds, Morwenna was screaming. "No! Get that out of my head!"

Kora turned to see Morwenna cover her face and whimper into the back of her chair. Arawn had gone stiff and pale, his white-rimmed eyes darted to Master Elwood. Kora noticed in alarm that his chest wasn't moving – he wasn't breathing.

"We warned you not to do that again," Master Elwood said in a harsh voice. "Now you know we can stop you, I'd advise you *never* to do something like this again."

Arawn nodded, but it was a stiff, barely noticeable movement of his head. Master Amyas nodded at Master Elwood. He returned the gesture and stopped whatever it was he was doing. Arawn collapsed back into his chair, colour returning to his face.

Kora looked worriedly at Luisella. Her best friend shared her discomfort. The rest of the lesson they were very subdued, not sending any images that might provoke the other to feel uncomfortable at all.

Chapter Nineteen

Later that evening, Kora heard a soft knock on her door. She opened it to Nyssa.

"Ready?" Nyssa asked, fixing her slippers.

"Nyssa, listen, I don't think this is such a good idea anymore," Kora hesitated. "Don't you think you've had enough extra practise?"

Nyssa looked hurt. "Lishe said you wouldn't want to keep practising with us once the novelty wore off. Don't come if you don't want to, but I'm going."

Kora hesitated, but then quickly ran after Nyssa. She could only imagine what Lishe would do tonight. Her imagination had clearly been sparked by Arawn's behviour. Kora didn't like the fascinated look in Lishe's eyes when she was looking at him.

In Lishe's room, Kora placed herself between Nyssa and her sister's disturbing friend. She knew Lishe understood, but she said nothing about it.

"Let's try what the masters were talking about today," Lishe said excitedly.

Kora frowned.

"What are you talking about?"

"Didn't you hear? They said they could stop him from using his powers. I want to figure out how."

"I don't think they'd want us to do that," Kora protested. "They would have taught us themselves if they wanted us to know."

"The masters don't teach us a lot of things," Lishe said with a wave of her hand. "I'm sure they expect us to experiment outside of class, otherwise why would they always tell Nyssa to practise more."

Kora fought the urge to hit Lishe. For all the progress Nyssa had made, it was still a sore point for her that she was not as skilled as she should be by this point in their training. They had all moved up to the advanced classes, but Nyssa always forgot things as soon as she had mastered the skill. It made her teachers fume in class and the other students laugh quietly behind their hands.

"Exactly what did you have in mind?" Kora asked tightly.

Lishe twisted a strand of her long black hair. "Well, remember that first time you joined us. I think we were close to it then. Let me show you."

Kora couldn't refuse. If she did, Lishe would try whatever she was thinking on Nyssa. For a moment, Kora felt an unreasonable surge of anger towards her sister. Nyssa was older than her. *She* should have been the one looking out for Kora, not the other way around. *Nyssa* should have been the one who was most skilled for having practised longer. But everyone in the entire castle, possibly the entire city, knew that Nyssa's gift was wasted on her. She had the potential to be a magnificent mistress if she had only dedicated more time to her studies when she was younger. Now, she was trying to catch up, but it was too little, too late – they would never accept her as a mistress when she had wasted so much time in her youth.

"Fine, but I want you to say everything you're doing out loud so that Nyssa knows what to do if something goes wrong."

Lishe smiled. "And so that *you* are prepared for what I am doing, no doubt."

Kora did not answer.

"Very well. I'm going to stretch my power out over you and try to enclose you within it. You've more power than me, so I'm sure it won't work, but I think it's the right idea. That would effectively stop you from using your power at all."

Kora stared at Lishe. "You've spent a lot of time thinking about this, haven't you?"

"Well, when a master makes such a comment in class, my mind always starts to work faster. Are you ready then?"

"I suppose so," Kora said slowly. She used that time to spread a thin layer of her power all around herself but pull her thoughts well within her wall. This time, there would be no way to avoid Lishe touching her power.

With a shudder, she felt Lishe's power crawling over hers, still as wispy as it had been before but constricting. It did not quite reach all over her. Kora found herself thankful that Lishe's power was limited.

For a moment, she thought Lishe was pulling her power back, but slowly realised she was simply focusing her power on one point. Lishe's power surrounded Kora's head, squeezing in tightly. No matter how Kora struggled from within, her trapped power could do nothing. Her heart beat faster, her vision darkened. With a jolt, Kora herself gasping for breath.

Kora gathered the power that was covering the rest of her body and ripped through Lishe's power, tearing it away.

"What are you doing?" Kora shouted, panting for air between words.

"I'm just trying to do what they did to Arawn in class," Lishe replied offhandedly.

"That's *not* what they did to him," Kora insisted. "They would not have let him suffocate!"

"What?" Nyssa asked in alarm. "What are you talking about?"

"Lishe had her power wound so tight around my head that I couldn't breathe. If I hadn't thrown her power off, I'd be unconscious by now."

"Lishe, please, we talked about this," Nyssa said softly. "You said you wouldn't do things like this to Kora anymore."

"To me?" Kora was incredulous. "What about to *you*?"

Nyssa looked down, shamefaced. Lishe held her head up proudly, with an arced eyebrow.

"That's it. Our practise session is over," Kora stated. "Nyssa, I want you to promise me that you won't practise with Lishe anymore."

"I ..." Nyssa looked between Lishe and Kora. Kora couldn't believe the hesitation.

"Nyssa!"

"Alright, I promise," she said quietly. "Sorry, Lishe."

"Not as sorry as you'll be one day when you're taken down by someone you could have defeated had you bothered to hone your skills. Just go."

Kora took Nyssa by the elbow and dragged her out of the room. She didn't let go until they were back in their hallway.

"Don't forget your promise, Nyssa," Kora told her. "No matter what happens, I never want you to practise alone with Lishe again."

Nyssa folded her arms across her chest. "I already promised, Kora. I don't have to listen to you. Just because we lost our mother, doesn't mean you need to act like one. I'm older than you. If anyone should be acting like our mother, *I* should."

Kora stared in dumbstruck silence as Nyssa walked gracefully down towards her chambers and disappeared behind the door. It was a slap in the face, one that she did not think she deserved. Kora shouldn't have been the more responsible one, Nyssa should have been. Kora shouldn't have been the more skilled one, Nyssa should have been. Unfortunately, Kora *was* both those things. She had never realised until now that Nyssa might be jealous of her because of it.

Chapter Twenty

~~Dear Father,~~
~~By the time you read this, I'll be gone. I don't want to tell you where I'm going~~
~~because I don't want you to follow me.~~

Kora scowled and twisted the quill between her fingers as she tried to find the right words.

~~I don't belong here anymore, so I'm going~~

She almost snarled in frustration as she screwed up the note and tossed it in the fireplace. Why was this so hard?

Dear Father,

I know we've had our differences in the past, and I know you'll disagree with my choice. It's why I didn't tell you before I made it. I hope you will understand, but I fear that you won't. Please try not to be angry and please don't blame anyone else for my decision to leave – it was mine and mine alone.

So many people disagree with my beliefs on how we should use our power – even you. I'm grateful to all the people who respect my views and keep their thoughts, manipulation and power to themselves, but I cannot live in a place where I feel I don't belong.

I don't know when I'll be back, or if I ever will. Know that I will love you always and will miss you terribly.

All my love to you,

Kora

Kora looked at her letter. She was not at all satisfied but could not think how to express herself any better. No matter what she wrote, her father would react badly. She couldn't blame him. She was leaving without giving him the chance to try to convince her to stay, no way for him to contact her, no clues as to where she was going.

I might never see him again.

She bit her lip and banished the thought. If she started down that track, she might not have the courage to leave at all. Kora left the letter, sealed with wax and her signet ring, on her desk. If she left her door unlocked, someone would be bound to find it. She debated writing a letter to her dearest friends and family, but knew she would not be able to find the words.

The door was locked, but Kora checked it again to make certain. She did not want to be interrupted in her final preparations. In her bedchamber, she pulled her rucksack out of her wardrobe – she had commissioned a new one after returning from the Outworld. Not letting herself think about that, she sorted through her clothes to find the most practical items, folded them and carefully packed the rucksack. For the past two days, she had sneaked extra food out of the dining hall and, that night, she had ordered up food to her room. All of it now went into her rucksack. She knew it would only last half a week at the most, but her rucksack was already close to bursting.

Yesterday, she'd stolen into her father's chambers when she knew he wasn't there and stuffed a small pouch with as many coins as she could. She was not blind to the fact that she had very few skills which could earn her money in the Outworld. Her needlework was mediocre at best, her kitchen skills left much to be desired. The only thing, other than using her powers, that she excelled at was reading and researching. She doubted those skills would serve her well in the Outworld.

Kora fastened the buckle on her rucksack. There was only one other thing she needed. Locked by a key she kept around her neck at all times, her desk drawer held a new little leather-bound book. Tucked safely in its pages were her notes that detailed how the paradises had been created, and Ophélie's original map. She knew Guiscard would be furious if he ever found out she'd torn out those pages, but she had not been able to duplicate the map precisely and she would need it if she was to have any hope of finding the paradises. She'd returned Ophélie's book to the library and had hidden it where she would be able to find it (if she ever returned) but where it was unlikely that anyone else, even Guiscard, would be unlikely to come across it.

Since that day she'd shown Uncle Lukys and Guiscard, and the librarian had leafed through Ophélie's book, they had not spoken about it with her. Kora was fairly sure they both suspected what she had decided to do, but she was likewise equally confident that neither of them would anticipate the timing of her departure. She doubted whether either of them would confess to her father that they had held any suspicion about her decision to leave. His fury was not worth incurring unless they could find her again and she was making sure that would be impossible.

Over the past two days, she'd managed to fashion a sash-belt with a hidden pouch to store the book. She tied the sash tightly around her waist and slipped the book into it. Satisfied it would not fall out, Kora covered it over with her shirt. The book was small enough that it would easily go unnoticed under the layers of cloth.

Kora shouldered the rucksack and looked around her chambers. There was nothing else she needed. It was time to go. Not wanting to risk a chance encounter in the castle hallways, she unlocked her door and walked over to the window overlooking the front courtyard of the castle island. She sat on the ledge and flipped her legs out and over. Any other lintep might be terrified by what she was about to do, but she was quite skilled now at traversing her invisible stairs.

Down in the courtyard, Kora stepped lightly over the grass. She could not risk being caught by the guards again. She couldn't even imagine what penalty she would pay if her intentions were discovered before she left. It didn't take her long to make her way from the island to the marketplace.

Without meaning to, her feet took her along the familiar route to Pér's house. She only realised what she was doing once she stood before his door.

That wooden door, painted with purple jacarandas, was so very familiar to her by now. She reached out and lightly traced the flowers with her fingertips. Would she ever come back to this comforting house again?

Kora turned away, pulling her power tightly behind her wall. Pér was too adept at sensing her presence. She could not allow him to see her tonight or he would insist on following her. She couldn't live with the heartbreak of a last kiss, nor the guilt if she gave in. She would not ruin his life simply because she could not bear to stay any longer.

It was not yet dawn when Kora reached the boundary. She turned and looked back at the large expanse of Illaria. She could not even see the castle from here. She doubted she would ever see it again. She had given herself a mission, but she did not truly believe that she could ask anyone in Illaria to help her if she discovered the truth.

Kora took a step towards the boundary. She had made her choice. It was time to leave. She pushed through the boundary and into the Outworld.